STORM

IRON ROGUES MC

FIONA DAVENPORT

STORM

When Blakely Evans' father was sent to prison for killing her kidnappers, he asked Gideon "Storm" Ayers to watch over her. Two years ago, the Iron Rogues' Road Captain realized Blakely was the woman who was meant to be his. But she was too young for Storm, so he protected her from afar, waiting for the day when he could finally claim her.

Only before he could come for Blakely, she was kicked out by the foster parents who'd promised him they would take care of her. Believing that Storm had deserted her, she was forced to run to her father's MC for help.

Now Storm is determined to deliver payback to the people who betrayed her. But his biggest obstacle will be earning back Blakely's trust.

PROLOGUE
STORM

"You asked to see me, Prez?"

I strolled into Cox's office and dropped onto one of the chairs in front of his desk. Cox was the president of the Iron Rogues Motorcycle Club and the father of one of my best friends.

I met Kye at a...questionably legal...drag race when I was a senior in high school. He'd been in college at Princeton University but had come down to my hometown in Florida for the races during spring break. I'd practically grown up in that world— a fuck you to my parents since they were basically useless and made it their mission in life to disapprove of everything I did anyway.

Fox and I hit it off and stayed in touch. The Iron Rogues pretty much ruled the underground racing world in Tennessee, Kentucky, Georgia, Alabama, and South Carolina. When Fox expressed an interest in expanding even farther south, I facilitated a partnership between the Iron Rogues and the man who bankrolled the majority of the races in Miami and the surrounding cities. Over the years, they'd taken control of the racing scene in the entire state and were creeping into Louisiana and Mississippi.

When I turned eighteen, I was willing to do pretty much anything to get the hell outta my town and away from my parents, so I joined the military. But I spent every leave with Kye—now Fox since he'd patched recently—and his family, which meant I spent most of my time at the MC.

Despite being absent so much, Cox let me prospect any time I was home. Whenever I decided to leave the service, I'd become a patched member of the club.

"Need a favor."

My brow shot up as I wondered what kind of favor this badass biker, who ran an entire club, would need from me.

"Fox tells me that you've been working in hostage negotiation."

I nodded. When I became a Ranger, I'd taken the mandatory Alternative Dispute Resolution—a fancy term for negotiation—two-hour course and excelled at it. So they'd put me through both of the weeklong courses. When I made Delta Force, it became my specialty. I didn't share that with many people, so I knew if Fox had told the prez, it was for a very good reason.

"Hate to take up your leave time, kid, but a friend of mine needs your skills. His twelve-year-old daughter's been kidnapped."

"Fuck." I frowned, leaning forward to rest my elbows on my knees.

"Saber's the president of the Westland Riders MC."

My brows shot up. "In my hometown?"

"Hell of a coincidence," Cox muttered with a nod.

The Westland Riders had a similar reputation to the Iron Rogues, but they were known to cross some lines that we wouldn't. "Saber pissed someone off enough for them to snatch his kid?"

"They want a ransom. WR is extremely successful at...what they do. And Saber already came from money when he patched. He dumped a huge portion of his inheritance into the MC coffers."

"They already received the ransom call?" Even if

I rode hard, I was still a ten-hour ride from where I grew up.

Cox shook his head. "Left a note in her backpack, which was found a block from the club. Said to expect a call in the next twenty-four hours."

"You have a file for me?" I assumed he'd give me as much information as he could so I would be able to familiarize myself with the situation and the players.

Cox picked up a yellow folder from his desk and held it out to me. "I'm sending Fox with you. He'll drive so you can look shit over. It'll also free you up if you need to get involved over the phone before arriving."

I lifted my chin in acknowledgment, my attention already on the dossier he'd provided. "Have Saber email me everything."

"Will do."

Twenty minutes later, Fox and I were on the road. I hated the idea of the little girl being in the hands of those assholes any longer than necessary, but trying to mediate from the truck would have been a fucking nightmare. So I was grateful they didn't receive the call before I arrived.

We pulled into the compound around four in the

morning, but there was no time for sleeping. I imme-diately got to work.

The call came a few hours later. Twenty million, and they expected Saber to deliver the money, then they would release Blakely within two hours.

My instincts were roaring, telling me they had no intention of letting her go. I talked them into sending a proof of life video, and when we received it, I cursed a blue streak. "She's not blindfolded."

Saber stared hard at the screen, seemingly unable to look away from his daughter's terrified expression. "What does that mean?"

I scrubbed my hands down my face and grunted in frustration. "It's likely that she's seen them."

"Motherfucker," Fox muttered, pacing away to glare out the window across the office.

Yeah, those fuckers had no intention of letting Blakely go.

When they called back, I managed to get them to agree to a place and time of our choosing for the money drop. They also agreed to show us a live feed of Blakely at the pickup. They would leave a cell phone for us to confirm, then we would be directed to leave the money and go.

During the conversation, I used tactics I'd mastered in my training and got them to admit to a few things that would aid us in figuring out who they were. After they hung up, I filled everyone in on what I learned and why the intel helped us.

Then we devised a plan.

I SLAMMED my foot against an exit door at the back of the warehouse and immediately put a bullet in the back of the guard's head. Some WR brothers came barreling in after me while several others barged in through the front entrance.

Trusting them to watch my back, I focused on finding the door—there it was.

I stayed along the perimeter of the large open space as I hurried to a door that matched the one behind Blakely in the video. The fuckers had been stupid enough to let us walk away with the phone connected to the live feed of their hostage. And their encryption on the signal was shit. A hacker friend of mine broke it in less than a minute, giving us the location where they were holding her.

The men who retrieved the money were in the wind, but the only thing any of us really cared about was Saber's little girl.

A man opened the door I was moving toward,

looking around wildly, obviously having heard the commotion outside. I raised my arm, and a second later, he dropped to the ground thanks to the small hole in his temple that trickled blood. I holstered my gun as I reached the room. The girl may have grown up around an MC, but I didn't know what her mental state was and wanted to appear as nonthreatening as possible.

She was huddled in the far corner of the room, half hidden by the metal cot on the wall next to her. Tears poured down her reddened cheeks, and her bangs were plastered to her damp forehead. The rest of her blond curls fell away from her face as she looked up at me, and my heart twisted at the terror filling her clear blue eyes.

As I approached, she suddenly sprang to her feet and slashed something in front of her, nearly slicing my stomach. "Get away from me!" she screamed. Then she whipped the weapon in front of her again, but I caught her wrist and grabbed the ...straightened mattress spring? *Clever girl.* I tossed it to the ground and yanked her into my arms. "Copperfield," I said loudly, so she would hear me over her screams. It was the codeword that Saber had given her so she would know the person using it was safe.

Her shouts and attempts to hit me ceased immediately. She seemed frozen as she stared up at me, and I could see her mind working, trying to decide whether she'd imagined what I had just said. "Copperfield," I murmured again.

A second later, she threw herself at me and hugged me so tight that it was almost painful as heaving sobs ripped from her chest.

"Your dad is here, Blakely," I told her softly as I picked her up and made my way to the door. Before I reached it, Saber came bursting into the room, and when he saw the girl in my arms, he dropped to his knees and sucked in a great big gulp of air.

"Blakely," he croaked as tears dripped from his eyes. Saber was a tough motherfucker. He ruled with an iron fist and could be lethal if necessary. But I wasn't surprised to see his display of emotion. It had been clear from the moment I met him how much he loved and adored his daughter.

"Daddy!" Blakely shouted and I quickly set her down so she could run into his embrace.

I made a hasty exit, not wanting to intrude on their reunion. Glancing around, I was relieved to see everyone we'd brought with us still breathing. Several of them stood in the center of the room talking while a few others dragged the dead bodies out the back door. Their fixer waited outside to collect them.

Fox's head lifted, and when he spotted me, he jerked his chin to the side to indicate that I should join them.

"We think we've got a location for the men who collected the money."

I was glad to hear it, but those guys were just lackeys. We needed to find the mastermind behind the kidnapping. "Any luck figuring out who they work for?"

Blakely

"BLAKELY. WAKE UP, SWEETHEART."

My dad's gritty voice penetrated my sleep, and I slowly woke. Knowing he was there stopped the panic from overtaking me, and I took a deep breath as my eyes fluttered, then opened. I'd been home almost a week, but I still had to remind myself that I was safe every time I woke up.

"Hey, there, ladybug," he greeted me with a strained smile.

"Daddy?" I struggled to sit up.

Gently, he helped me into a sitting position, then smoothed my hair back away from my face.

"I love you more than anything. You know that, right?"

I smiled and nodded. "I love you too, Daddy." Glancing around my room, I frowned when I realized the sun hadn't come up yet. "What time is it?"

"Early, sweetheart. I...I just needed to see you and..." He sighed and scrubbed his face with his hands. "I just...I couldn't let it go, Blakely. They had to be punished."

"What?" I was confused by what he was saying, but something in his tone and expression had the panic threatening to cut off my air again.

"I couldn't take the risk that they would come for you again, ladybug. Even if it meant not seeing you grow up."

"What?" My voice hit a high pitch, and my heart beat hard against my ribs. "What do you mean? Daddy—"

"Saber." A deep voice from the doorway interrupted me. A voice I'd come to know well since I'd been brought home. One that made me feel safe and happy.

Gideon took a step inside, and his face softened

when he looked at me. But unlike most times when he saw me, his lips didn't curve into a playful smile.

His brown eyes shifted to my dad, and he grunted, "They're here."

"I need you to stay here, sweetheart," my dad said, his tone earnest.

"But—"

"No buts, Blakely. Promise me that you will stay in your room until the sun comes up." I opened my mouth, but he gently grabbed my arms and demanded, "Promise me."

"I'll stay with you, Blakely," Gideon told me.

"Okay," I whispered.

My dad kissed my forehead and gave me a tight hug. "I love you, ladybug. Never forget that."

"I love you too, Daddy." I didn't know what was going on, but I knew something was wrong. A feeling of dread settled over me.

He stood and faced Gideon. "You promised you'd take care of her," Dad said.

"You have my word." Gideon tilted his head to the side and studied my dad for a moment. "I will make sure she's protected and taken care of, but it's not me she needs, Saber. She needs her dad."

My dad inhaled raggedly, his shoulders slumping

forward. "I just...I couldn't let them get away with it."

Gideon's voice was low when he replied, but the room was so quiet that I still managed to hear him. "And now she's paying for it all over again."

"I know..." My dad sighed and glanced over at me; his blue eyes, like mine, filled with something sad. "Love you, ladybug. I hope you can forgive me."

Then he stalked out of the room. I threw my covers off and hurried to follow him, but Gideon scooped me into his arms and moved to the rocking chair by the head of my bed, then sat down, keeping me cuddled in his arms.

"You promised, Blakely," he murmured.

"He's not coming back, is he?" I sniffed as my throat clogged and my vision blurred.

"No."

"I'm going to be all alone."

Gideon put a finger under my chin and gently lifted my head. "I won't always be right by your side, Blakely. But you aren't alone. I'll always be there for you. Always."

Something in the way he promised me so fiercely helped to soothe my fear. I believed him. Gideon would never let me feel all alone.

1

BLAKELY

The light barely streamed between the slats of the blinds in my bedroom when I rolled over with a groan at the knock on my bedroom door. "Yeah?"

"Time to get up, Blakely. Pancakes are ready," my foster mother called.

"Okay."

Flinging the covers off, I sighed as I climbed out of bed. One of the best parts of winter break was being able to sleep in, but I knew I wouldn't get the chance to today.

While everyone else was excited to get up early to open presents, I didn't have much to look forward to. I'd been lucky with my foster home placement, but Christmas morning had lost much of its meaning after my dad went to prison. The Davidsons were nice enough to me, but they didn't exactly go all out on holidays. At least not for me. Their son was a different story.

Bryan was a twenty-four-year-old senior in college, but they still treated him like a little kid. Patti drove four hours twice a month to do his laundry and restock his fridge and freezer with home-cooked food. She kept a calendar of his assignments and reminded him when everything was due, even helping to finish the ones he didn't bother doing. Not that I blamed her that much when her son was in his sixth year of college with his parents paying the entire way. She had to be chomping at the bit for him to finally graduate.

Since they had a whole lot more to look forward to than I did, everyone was already seated at the kitchen table when I made it downstairs.

Bryan scooted out the chair next to him. "Merry Christmas, birthday girl."

I'd always gotten a weird vibe from him, but at least he'd already moved to college before his parents took me in. He'd been in an off-campus apartment since his sophomore year, so he didn't come home for summers. This meant that I usually only had to put up with him during holidays, thank goodness.

"Umm, thanks."

Patti's brows drew together as her gaze darted between her son and me. She shot her husband a worried look, but he just shrugged. My foster father wasn't much of a talker, but I liked that about him.

After we finished breakfast, I did the dishes while Bryan started opening his presents. He still had a huge stack to go through when I wandered into the living room. Instead of reaching for one of his, though, he handed me a package from under the tree. "Here, this one's for you, Blakely."

In all of the holidays I had spent with his family, Bryan had never gone out of his way to make me feel included, so I found it odd that he was being so nice to me today. I felt uncomfortable as I reached out to grab the wrapped gift, muttering, "Thanks."

His gaze drifted toward my chest as he murmured, "You're welcome."

I padded across the room to sit as far away from him as I could while I opened my present, a pair of pajamas. Patti didn't give him the chance to hand me the other two gifts she and Scott had gotten for me, which I appreciated because I didn't want her son anywhere near me.

Unfortunately, my luck ran out later in the afternoon when Bryan stepped into my bedroom, where

I'd been hiding out ever since we finished eating lunch. Swinging my legs over the edge of my bed, I asked, "What're you doing?"

"Making my move." His gaze slid down to my boobs, and he licked his lips. "Been waiting a long time for you to finally be legal."

Gulping down the lump in my throat as I crossed my arms over my chest, I shook my head. "I don't understand."

"Pretend as much as you want, but I've seen the hot looks you've given me every time I came home." He shut the door behind him and flipped the lock on the knob, totally freaking me out. "Now that you're eighteen, I can finally give you what you've been asking for all this time."

Shaking my head, I hopped to my feet. "I don't know what you're talking about, Bryan. I swear, I've never looked at you as anything other than the son of my foster parents."

"Kinky." He wagged his brows. "If you wanna call me your brother while I'm pounding you into the mattress, that works for me."

My stomach churned, and I made a gagging noise. "That's never going to happen."

"Wrong," he growled, prowling toward me.

"You're what I want for Christmas, and we both know that I always get what I want."

"You can't just—"

My words were swallowed by a gasp when Bryan wrapped his fingers around my wrist in a grip tight enough to leave a bruise and yanked me off balance. I stumbled into his body and pushed my palms against his chest, making him back up a few steps. Then I jerked back, trying to pull away from his hold. I cried out when he wrenched my arm toward him. "Stop!"

Patti pounded on the door and yelled, "Why is this locked? What's happening in there?"

"You better let go," I warned. "I might be eighteen now, but that doesn't make what you were about to do legal."

"Open this door right this minute or else," Patti threatened from the hallway.

I narrowed my eyes at Bryan. "You heard her."

"This isn't gonna go how you think it is." Releasing my arm, he smirked at me. "You should've just given me what I wanted without kicking up a fuss."

Free of his hold, I stomped over to the door, flipped the lock, and yanked it open. Patti shoved past me, and as soon as she spotted her son, she shrieked, "I knew it!"

"I'm sorry, Mom."

I whirled around, shocked that Bryan was so quick to apologize for what he'd done, but I was stunned to see that he'd yanked open the top three buttons on his shirt and ruffled his hair. Patti arrived just in time to make sure nothing happened—thank goodness—but Bryan proceeded to lie his butt off.

"I was trying to let Blakely down easy, but I never should have let her drag me into her bedroom." He shook his head with a rueful sigh. "I don't know how, but I must've given her the impression that I was interested in her as more than just my foster sister. She wanted to, umm...you know...umm..."

The jerk had the nerve to pretend to be too embarrassed to explain how I hit on him when he was lying through his teeth.

"What?" I shook my head. "That's not at all—"

Patti didn't let me finish explaining before she gripped my arm in the same spot where her son had grabbed me. I winced and cried out, but she didn't care that she was hurting me. "I should have known that you would try to get your filthy hands on my boy. I tried my best to raise you right, but it was already too late when you came to us. Dirty biker sluts like you don't know any better than to use your feminine wiles to try to get what you want. You're not going to ruin my son's life on my watch. Pack your stuff and get the hell out of my house."

"But you said I could stay until after graduation," I protested.

"That was before you tried to seduce my baby boy," she hissed. "You have ten minutes before I call the police and tell them you're trespassing."

"Told you," Bryan murmured as he strutted past me.

Nine minutes later, my heart was heavy as I stumbled out of the house that I had called home for the past six years. I had no plan for where to go since I'd expected to stay for five more months. Unlike most kids in the system, my foster parents hadn't been in a rush to kick me out when I aged out. Not until their jerk of a son got butt hurt and wanted me out of their house. On freaking Christmas Day. Barely a week after my eighteenth birthday.

After I tossed the last of my bags into the back of my truck—which I treasured because it was the last time I'd really felt as though Storm cared about me— I climbed into the driver's seat and rested my head against the steering wheel. "What am I going to do?"

Checking into a decent hotel wouldn't be easy

between my age and lack of a credit card. And I couldn't call my dad because the jail had specific hours when prisoners could use the phones.

Bryan stepped onto the front porch, crossing his arms over his chest as his lips curved into a smirk. The part of me that was my father's daughter wanted to get out of my truck so I could go kick his butt, but I knew it wouldn't accomplish anything except for me getting arrested. I needed somewhere to sleep...but not badly enough to wind up in jail.

Pressing my lips together as I heaved a deep sigh through my nose, I started the engine and backed out of the driveway. I drove aimlessly for about an hour before it finally dawned on me where I could go.

The Westland Riders' VP, Jagger, was running the club since my dad couldn't do it from jail for the long term. But from what he'd said during my visits—which I'd had to keep a secret from my foster parents—the guys refused to replace him because they continued to think of my dad as their true leader.

I hadn't been around any of them much since he went to prison because Patti was not a fan of bikers, but that didn't mean the club didn't still see me as family. If I showed up at the gate of the compound where I'd spent so much time growing up, they would take me in.

If Storm had kept the promise that he'd made to me all those years ago, I'd have another option. But he hadn't been there for me since he'd gotten out of the military. Heck, I'd barely spoken with him over the past two years. So much for not leaving me alone just like everyone else in my life had done.

2

STORM

"Storm."

Fox stepped out of his office and pointed at me, then crooked his fingers.

I set down my drink on the wooden top of the long bar that took up one side of the lounge in the clubhouse.

He was seated behind his desk when I entered, and he pointed at one of the chairs in front. "Sit."

Raising a brow, I did as directed. "Something wrong, Prez?"

After getting bored working on Wall Street, Fox had taken over for his dad several years ago. He was a damn good leader, and we were all as loyal to him as we had been to his father.

"I need you to hear me out before you flip your shit."

My eyes narrowed, and I sat up straighter in the chair.

"I just got a call from the Westland Riders VP."

Fox's tone was wary, and I bit back the instinct to shout at him to tell me what the fuck was going on. The brothers in the WR kept an eye on Blakely for me, so we touched base once a week. They were supposed to call me if there was even the slightest hiccup in her life. So why had they called Fox instead?

I was already on edge because Blakely had turned eighteen a week ago, and I hadn't been able to go get her yet. Guilt trickled through me because the reason I was still at home was that my younger sister, Elise, had come to spend her Christmas break with me. It was the first time I'd talked her into leaving the town where we grew up, and I wasn't gonna ditch her like I'd done when I turned eighteen.

My plan had been to show up the day of Blakely's birthday and be back in time to spend the holiday with my sister. But Elise had shown up early, hoping to work at one of the Iron Rogue's businesses for a couple of weeks. I'd fought her on the idea since I had plenty of money to take care of her. But Elise was as stubborn as I was, so I finally gave in before she resorted to tears.

She was going back to school in a week, so I was doing my best not to go fucking crazy until I could finally go retrieve my woman.

"Something happened with Blakely."

Fox's statement penetrated my thoughts, and I shot to my feet. "What the fuck?" I bellowed.

"Sit your ass down, Storm, and let me give you all the fucking information," Fox ordered.

I bit back a scathing response and dropped back onto my seat, wondering if smoke was literally coming out of my ears.

He gave me a brief rundown of what they'd told him occurred with Blakely's foster brother, and my temper burned hotter.

"Why the fuck didn't they call me?" I asked through clenched teeth.

Fox sighed and scratched his cheek. "They are planning to go after the little shit in a couple of days. They knew you'd tell them to wait—"

"Those motherfuckers called you because they don't answer to you." Fox nodded. "But since Saber put me in charge of Blakely, everything concerning her goes through me."

"I told them to back the fuck off and call you, but

I don't know if they'll listen to my advice. I just got off the phone with them ten minutes ago, so you should have some time to get things in order. Assuming they don't do anything stupid before then. I'm sending you on the run tomorrow since it's near her town. Take whatever time you need to handle shit."

"Fucking hell," I grunted. "I—" I'd been so focused on the incident that her living situation hadn't sunk in until right that moment. "They kicked her out?"

"Yeah," he acknowledged.

"Where is she staying?"

Prez sighed and gave me a look that told me to keep a lid on my temper, which meant I was gonna be fucking pissed when he confirmed my suspicions. "At the clubhouse."

"Son of a bitch!" I roared, jumping to my feet. "I'm—"

My cell phone rang, and I yanked it from my pocket, ready to rip the WR VP a new asshole, but it was one of my club brothers. "What?" I snarled.

"You better get your ass out to the garage," Whiskey growled. "Your sister was in an accident."

"Elise!" I shouted at Fox as I jumped up and took off running.

Fox WAITED for several brothers to arrive, making me want to put a fist through the wall to vent my impatience. Maverick, our VP, stood just beside him, arms crossed, feet apart, looking just as intimidating as he really was. Viper, Savage, Deviant, Blade, Ice, and Whiskey all came in and found various seats.

I'd asked for a meeting while we were eating Christmas dinner because this shit couldn't wait.

"What happened?" Fox asked.

I explained how my sister had happened upon a drug deal in the parking lot of our bar, Midnight Rebel, and the subsequent chase that had ended up with her car being run off the road. The tension in the room became deadly.

The Iron Rogues had our own brand of justice... usually outside the laws of the land. We had all kinds of dirt and blood on our hands, but we didn't tolerate drugs. In any situation. The first time any member was caught using, they were given the choice of rehab or leaving the MC. There were no second chances. Our zero tolerance for drugs was no secret, either.

We sure as fuck didn't allow them in or around our businesses. In order to keep that shit off the streets, we'd even assisted local law enforcement in busting up some drug rings in the area. Unofficially.

So the fact that this asshole had not only violated our rules concerning drugs but then also attempted to kill an innocent woman to avoid being caught, had every one of us itching to put a bullet in the asshole. Especially since Elise was automatically under the protection of the club because she was my sister.

I was fucking livid and determined to do whatever it took to make sure that meth head ate a bullet for what he'd done.

Fox's dark gaze landed on Deviant. "Have Savage send over the security footage. Do whatever you have to. Get me a motherfucking name."

Deviant nodded.

"I can comb the security footage," I volunteered.

Fox held up his hand, cutting off whatever I might have been about to say next. "You have to leave on a run tomorrow."

I blinked, then guilt flooded me as I silently cursed. How the fuck had I forgotten? "Right. Shit. Can't believe I forgot." I ran my hands through my hair, exhaling raggedly as I felt myself being torn apart. Blakely was my woman. She needed me. So did Elise, though. FUCK!! "But my sister—"

"She's got all of us, brother," Mav piped up reassuringly. "You know every one of us will protect her with our life. And we'll let you know as soon as we have something to go on."

"I'll come right back," I swore.

Fox shook his head. "No. Focus on the run and on your woman. If shit hasn't been handled when you get back, we'll get you up to speed and let you handle the asshole. Blakely comes first. You've waited long enough, and that situation could blow the fuck up any day."

Every brother in the room nodded, and I felt a small measure of relief. They would all be on top of Elise's situation, but I was the only one who could handle Blakely's.

We strategized for a bit longer, then rejoined the families for the rest of the night. I attempted to set things aside and be in a good mood so I didn't ruin my sister's holiday. But I couldn't help counting down the hours until I would leave to go get my girl. And I'd made sure to put in a call to Jagger, the WR VP, to make it clear that if anyone touched Blakely, I would put the son of a bitch in the ground. I also managed to drag a promise from him that they wouldn't deal with her foster brother until I got there.

In the morning, I warned my brothers to take

care of my sister and to also stay the fuck away from her—much to Elise's irritation. But that was what big brothers were for.

When I met Viper out in the garage, he was waiting on his bike, ready to go.

"Blakely know you're coming?" he asked, watching me curiously.

I shook my head as I did a quick check to make sure everything on my hog was good to go. "Don't think she's particularly happy with me, and I don't want her taking off and putting herself into a dangerous situation."

Viper swung his leg over the seat and cocked his head to the side. "'Cause you stayed away?"

"Yeah." Our phone calls over the past several months had been stilted. I knew why...but I couldn't figure out any other way to handle the situation.

"She'll understand once you explain."

I didn't respond out loud. Just started my bike and rolled out.

I fucking hoped she got why I handled the situation the way I did. Not that it would change anything. I would still be claiming her. If Blakely didn't want to listen, then she was gonna find herself tied to our bed while I convinced her to forgive me with my mouth on her pussy.

While Blakely was growing up, I had been a steady fixture in her life, just like I was in my sister's. But it wasn't often in person since I was in the service. I visited them when I could and stayed in touch with phone calls and video chats.

Unfortunately, Blakely had been forced to go into the foster care system after her dad was sent to prison for killing the men involved in her kidnapping. I'd understood his need for vengeance, but I'd been pissed as fuck when he let it cloud his judgment and the jackass got caught.

Through smart decisions with my money—and a lack of bills while in the service—I had enough for my children and my children's children to live comfortably. Which made it slightly easier to be away because I made sure her foster family had plenty of money to care for her. And if the reports filed were anything but glowing, they'd not only lose what I was sending them but I also made sure they knew I'd burn their lives to the ground.

I left the Army two years ago, and my first stop was to see Blakely. When I pulled up to the house, she ran out the door and threw herself into my arms. It was the first time I'd seen her in person for nearly a year, and somehow, despite our video chats, it had escaped my notice that she had grown into a woman.

But when my arms closed around her, and I felt her soft curves and her cinnamon scent wafted to my nose, I became instantly aware of what I'd missed.

Blakely was too young for me to be having the kind of thoughts that started sifting through my mind. And I knew that if I didn't keep my distance, I was gonna do something monumentally stupid. There was no way in hell that I would risk anything taking me away from her. She'd already lost too much.

So I took her to dinner, then made a hasty exit. The hurt in her eyes as I said goodbye almost broke my resolve.

The next day, I went to see her dad in prison. I gave him every excuse I could think of—that didn't involve my attraction to his daughter—and asked him to let me find someone else to watch out for her.

He'd listened quietly, observing me in a way I couldn't figure out.

Then he shook his head and told me he didn't trust anyone else. He reminded me of my promise and suggested I protect her from afar. Stay around her life, but not in it.

I almost said no...but when I thought about Blakely being taken care of by anyone other than me, fury burned inside me.

I decided if he wasn't going to let me out of my oath, then he would have to deal with the consequences.

I left the prison, and while it nearly tore my heart out to stay away from Blakely, I reassured myself that I would come for her in two years.

And that day was finally here.

We parked our bikes around the back when we arrived at the Westland Riders MC. The MC was less than a third of the size of the Iron Rogues, so they didn't have a secure compound like we did. Their clubhouse was a former boarding house in the small town's downtown area.

After securing my hog, I bounded up the three steps to the entrance and shoved the door open.

The lighting was low, but I could see every detail as my eyes swept over the room. It was long and narrow, with multiple seating areas along one wall. On the other were pool tables and arcade games, as well as a long bar. A couple of guys were lounging on couches and watching a mounted television. Their heads whipped in my direction, their hands reaching for weapons. But when they saw me, they slouched back into their seats.

Jagger walked in through a swinging doorway, and when he spotted me, he jerked his chin toward the direction he'd come from. "Kitchen," he muttered, then hastily stepped to the side so he wouldn't be knocked over when I stalked past him.

The door led to a decent-sized industrial kitchen, and two women stood near the appliances, chatting and drinking from mugs. I dismissed them immediately and looked at the long table across the room.

My breath got caught in my throat, and my heart thudded so hard it was painful.

Silky blond curls were tied up in a cute ponytail, but little tendrils had escaped and framed Blakely's heart-shaped face. Her big blue eyes widened when she caught sight of me, and her coal-black lashes fluttered as her pink lips formed a little O.

She stood, and my eyes continued down, slowly perusing her body now that I had given myself permission to appreciate it. Blakely had a slender build but with curves in all the right places.

Her tits were on the smaller side, but they were round and perky, and I knew they would fill my hands perfectly. A narrow waist led to the sweet flare of her hips, and I swallowed hard when I saw her seemingly endless legs. She wore shorts, and with all that skin on display, I hardened at the thought of how it would feel to have all that softness wrapped around my head.

When my gaze finally returned to her face, the surprise had been replaced with wariness. Her eyes were narrowed, and her lips pursed as she cocked her head to the side.

"What are you doing here, Storm?" she asked, her tone carefully neutral.

"I came for you, baby."

3

BLAKELY

My breath caught in my chest at the intense look in his dark brown eyes, and I didn't like how much Storm still got to me after all this time. He would always have a place in my heart for everything he had done for me when I was kidnapped and for about four years afterward, but he was the last person I expected to see at the Westland Riders MC clubhouse. The man had practically avoided me like the plague for the past two years, so what in the heck was he doing here, saying crap like that? And what was up with him using a term of endearment like "baby" when talking to me?

Torn between the desire to get up and throw myself in his arms or to stay right where I was and give him the silent treatment, I pressed my lips into a flat line while I lamented the fact that he was hotter than ever.

He'd added a lot of muscle to his tall frame since the last time I'd seen him. His dark brown hair was a little longer, and my fingers itched to push back a lock that had fallen onto his forehead. His beard and mustache were cropped short and only accentuated his plush lips. And seeing the new tattoo on his neck —a black skull with red eyes, nose, and mouth—made me wonder how much other ink he'd added to his sexy body since I'd last seen him.

But just because Storm made me feel as though my panties were about to spontaneously combust didn't mean that I was going to welcome him with open arms. Not after all this time.

Getting to my feet, I planted my fists on my hips. "You came for *me*? What does that even mean?"

"Not sure I can be any clearer, baby." His lips curved into a cocky smile that somehow irritated me but also made him hotter. "I don't make a habit outta dropping into another club's compound without a damn good reason. You're here, so I'm here."

Butterflies swarmed in my belly at his declaration, but it would take more than some pretty words for me to forgive him for leaving me alone for so long. "If that were true, you would've been around more over the past two years. Or like...at all. Instead of breaking your promise and basically abandoning me."

"I'm so fucking sorry, Blakely." He took a couple of steps toward me but stopped when I held up my hands. "You gotta know that I wouldn't have stayed away without a damn good reason."

"Yup, I totally thought that," I conceded, shaking my head when he took that to mean he could come closer. "For maybe the first six months or so. But then I noticed you also hardly ever called, and I couldn't come up with a decent excuse for that. Except that once you got out of the military, you realized you didn't want to deal with the hassle of having me around because you wanted to get on with your life."

"I've never thought of you as a hassle." He closed the distance between us and took my hands in his. "And I missed you every damn day since I last saw you."

"Missed me? Right." I snorted while rolling my eyes. "So much that you've stayed away since my sixteenth birthday, and I haven't heard from you besides a couple of five-minute conversations in months. Those are definitely the actions of a guy who wants to be around me."

The sarcasm was thick in my voice, but Storm

didn't seem to take offense. Instead, he flashed me an apologetic smile and squeezed my hands. "I get that you're upset, but—"

"Gee, thanks for being so understanding." I huffed out a laugh that held no humor. "But for the record, I'm not upset. I'm angry. There's a difference."

"And you have every reason to be pissed." Storm released one of my hands to rake his fingers through his hair. "At a lot of fucking people, me included."

"You're right. There's plenty of anger to go around," I agreed with a sigh. "But hey, at least the truck you gave me the last time you bothered to come around came in handy yesterday. I guess I owe you some gratitude for the fact that I was able to make it here when my foster parents kicked me out of their house because they can't admit that their son is a creep."

Storm dropped his arm to his side, his nostrils flaring as he fisted his hand. "Don't worry, that bastard is gonna pay for what he tried to do to you. Same with your foster parents for fucking you over."

"Stop." This time, I was the one who reached for his hands to give them a squeeze as I shook my head. "I already told Jagger that I didn't want anyone doing something stupid on my behalf. The last thing

I need is for someone else to go to jail because of me."

"You are not to blame for what your dad did," he grumbled, taking advantage of our position to wrap his fingers around my wrist and tug me closer. "Not a damn part of that fiasco was on you. Those bastards deserved what they got, and your dad fucking up with how he took care of them is on him. Not you."

Logically, I knew he was right. But the little girl inside me who'd lost her only remaining parent still felt guilty that he'd been sent to prison because I had been taken. "That doesn't change the fact that I don't want anyone to get in trouble on my behalf. Not even you, Storm."

His plush lips firmed into a flat line as he narrowed his eyes at me. "I'm Gideon to you, baby."

"You were Gideon back when I could trust you to stick around." I swallowed the lump in my throat before adding, "But you proved me wrong with your disappearing act over the past couple of years. So now you're Storm."

"After we talk, you're gonna understand why I had to stay away and why I'll always be Gideon to you. But we're not having this conversation here in front of an audience."

I glanced over at the old ladies who'd been

cleaning up after dinner and found them leaning against the counter, unabashedly staring at us. I heaved a deep sigh when Staci—their tail gunner's woman—winked at me. Turning to Storm, I muttered, "I guess we can go talk in my room."

"Not your room," he growled. "Just the one you used for the nights you're spending here."

"Pardon?" I asked, my brows drawing together.

"You sure you want to go upstairs with him?" Staci shook her head with a laugh. "Because I have a feeling you're going to have your hands full with this one, honey."

Storm shot her a warning look, and Angela, one of the enforcer's old ladies, elbowed her in the side. Then without any warning, he crouched down to put his shoulder in my stomach and gently lifted me off my feet.

"What are you doing?" I shrieked, clutching Storm's Iron Rogues cut while he stomped out of the kitchen to whistles from the guys hanging out by the bar.

"Which room did you give her?"

I lifted my head to glare at Jagger when he answered, "Take a left at the top of the stairs. Last room on the right. No matter how often he said we should, we never emptied Saber's room. Seemed like the right place to put his daughter until you could come and collect her. Figured you'd be fast once you heard she was here, but with Christmas being just yesterday, I thought it'd take you a couple of days to make it down here."

My brows drew together as I wondered why my dad's VP thought that Storm wanted anything to do with me, let alone that he'd come running when he heard I was at their clubhouse. I hoped Storm had a good explanation for what was happening because nothing had made sense since he strode into the kitchen.

As soon as he set me on my feet—after kicking the door shut behind us so we'd have privacy—I planted my hands at my hips and scowled up at him. "That was not okay, Storm. You can't just show up in my life after two years and act as though you belong there."

"You might not have seen me, but I never left your life, baby," he swore, sincerity shining from his dark eyes.

"Why did you avoid me so much, then? I understood when I was younger because you were in the military, but you've been out for two years, and I've barely seen you."

I squeezed my eyes shut when my voice cracked

at the end, but they popped back open when he scooped me into his arms again and set me on the chair in the corner of the room. Then he blew me away when he explained, "Because I didn't want to end up next to your dad in jail, where he'd kill me for doing all the dirty things that come to mind when I look at you."

When Bryan had said something similar, it'd been creepy. But hearing those words coming out of Storm's mouth—something I had fantasized about many times—had me pressing my thighs together to ease the sudden ache in my core.

4

———

STORM

"D-dirty?" Blakely practically squeaked. Her face was flushed, and I grinned when she shifted on the chair, uncrossing and re-crossing her legs.

"Yeah, baby," I murmured, leaning down to put a hand on each armrest, caging her in and bringing our faces practically nose to nose. "You have no idea how many times I thought about kissing your pretty mouth, seeing those pink lips wrapped tight around my cock, burying my face in your sweet pussy and eating until I was stuffed. How often I dreamed of popping your cherry and filling your tight little virgin pussy with my fat cock until you were screaming my name while I claimed you."

Blakely's breaths were shallow and choppy,

making her delectable tits bounce. The sweet blush covering her cheeks had spread down under the collar of her T-shirt, and I tightened my hold on the chair arms to keep from tearing it off so I could see just how far down the color had spread.

"How do you know I'm a—"

Chuckling darkly, I dipped my head to the side and ran my nose along her cheek, inhaling her delicious cinnamon scent until I reached her ear. "I always had eyes on you, baby. And if any little fucker had touched you, I'd have sent someone to make sure they never did it again."

Blakely gasped as her head reared back. "You're the reason none of the guys at my school ever asked me on a date?" she snapped.

I grinned, completely unrepentant. "Those little shits weren't anywhere near good enough for you."

"Oh?" Her tone was indignant, and she looked so damn cute that I had to swallow a smile. "And just who is?"

I sobered and probed her blue eyes with mine, answering, "Nobody, Blakely. Not one person out there is worthy of you, including me. But I don't give a fuck. Maybe that makes me a complete bastard, but I'm claiming you. You are mine."

"Yours?" she breathed, blinking rapidly as her blue orbs darkened with desire.

"Mine," I muttered right before I grabbed her waist and lifted her onto her feet.

A shot of triumph streaked through me when Blakely immediately melted into me as I wrapped my arms around her. When I nipped her full bottom lip, she let out a little gasp, allowing me to slip my tongue in to taste her. Her delicious flavor pulled a groan from deep in my chest, and I moved my hands up to her neck, using both thumbs to press on her chin, opening her up even more. Then I angled my head and took the kiss deeper.

My dreams of her didn't come anywhere close to the perfection of having her subtle curves pressed against me as her mouth moved against mine.

"It was fucking hell to stay away from you, baby," I grunted before nipping her bottom lip again. Then I placed hot, wet kisses along her jaw, moving down to the side of her neck. "But I knew I'd never be able to keep my hands off you. And I swore that I would always be there for you." I leaned my head back so I could stare into her beautiful blue eyes when I continued, "I know you're having a hard time believing it, but I never left you alone, baby. Like I said, if I wasn't watching over you, then I had someone I trusted making sure you were safe and had everything you needed."

Her gaze softened a little, and I rested my forehead against hers. "I knew that when I came for you, I'd never let you go, and I wasn't willing to risk breaking my promise."

"I wish you'd told me," she whispered.

I leaned back again to study her face. "You know why I couldn't, Blakely."

Her cheeks bloomed red, and she lowered her gaze to my chest. "I...I don't know what you're talking about."

I grinned and cupped her cheeks, rubbing my thumb over the pink spots. "Yes, you do, baby. You think I didn't notice how you looked at me the last time we saw each other? The way your breath hitched when my hands brushed against your skin? How you licked your pretty lips every time your gaze dropped to my mouth?"

Blakely's blush deepened, making me wonder how her skin would look when I made her come. "Can you blame me? You were seriously hot, Storm. And you know it," she muttered.

"Was? I'm not hot now?"

Her lips pressed together as she tried to hold

back a smile and attempted to look indifferent. "I hadn't noticed."

"Liar." My smile turned wicked as I bent my head so our lips brushed when I next spoke. "Gonna show you how fucking hot we'll burn, baby."

I sipped at her lips for a moment before kissing her deeply. She mewled when my tongue slid against hers. The little sounds of pleasure she made were driving me to distraction, making me crave more of them. I glided my palms down her throat to her torso and cupped her plump tits.

I gave the mounds a gentle squeeze while my lips trailed up her silky skin to just below her ear. "Perfect," I crooned. "One of these days, I'm gonna fuck these sexy tits."

She shivered, and I felt the hard peaks of her nipples digging into my palms through her shirt, making me growl as desire flooded my body. I needed to get my mouth on her more than I needed to breathe.

I grabbed the hem of her T-shirt and slid it up, then grunted in approval when she raised her arms so I could whip the material over her head. Her sexy as fuck tits were half covered by blue lace, the exposed part jiggling with each of her choppy breaths. A surge of desire coursed through me, and I palmed the sweet mounds, rubbing my thumbs over the hard peaks. A whimper escaped her lips as I leaned down and brushed my mouth over the swells of her breasts.

"So damn gorgeous," I rasped in a husky voice. Every muscle in my body was tense as I fought the urge to throw her on the bed and fuck her hard and deep. It was gonna happen, but not before I made sure she was ready. I hated the thought of hurting her, and that thought gave me the strength to stay in control.

"I've been waiting for this moment for so damn long, baby."

"I..." Blakely paused, and I looked up, meeting her hesitant gaze. I smiled encouragingly, and it seemed to bolster her confidence because her voice was stronger when she continued. "I dreamed of this. Of you. Coming for me. Taking me." She double blinked, then shook her head. "Honestly, I'm still wondering if this is real or I'm back in my dreams."

"Oh, this is definitely real, baby," I grunted before dropping to my knees. Then I captured one of her nipples through the fabric of her bra, and she gasped. Her hands tangled in my hair, and the pinch of pain when she tugged the strands only fueled my hunger for her.

"Storm," she whimpered.

I retreated a few inches and scowled up at her. "Gideon, Blakely," I growled. "You call me Gideon."

She blinked a few times, trying to focus on me. Then she nodded and whispered, "Gideon."

Heat flared in her gorgeous blue eyes, driving me just a little bit closer to losing my mind. I hooked my fingers under the fabric of her bra and peeled it away. My cock had been hard since the moment I saw her in the kitchen earlier, and my shaft continued to stiffen as I explored her mouth and body.

When her tits spilled free, my dick swelled even more, painfully stretching the skin. I was leaking come and probably making a fucking mess in my pants. But I didn't give a shit because her rosy nipples were begging for my attention.

Wrapping my lips around one, I sucked the stiffened peak gently before scraping it with my teeth and taking a deep pull. Blakely moaned, her body quivering as she arched her back, looking sexy as fuck.

I gave the opposite tip the same treatment while my hands glided around to unhook her bra. After releasing her nipple with a pop, I kissed each peak, then pushed to my feet. I stared into her passion-glazed eyes while sliding the fabric down her arms and dropping it to the floor. Then I filled my hands with her plump globes and bent my head to take her mouth once more. She shivered and moaned while my fingers twisted and plucked at her sensitive buds.

Blakely clutched my biceps for a few minutes, but then she tentatively moved her hands to my chest, playing with the sides of my cut. "Gideon?" she whispered against my lips.

I released her mouth and drew my head back, gazing down at her. "Yeah, baby?"

I grinned when pink spots bloomed on her cheeks. She was going to have to ask me for what she wanted.

"Well, um...it doesn't really seem fair that I don't, um, have a shirt on, and you're still wearing so many clothes."

My smile widened, and I winked at her. "Sounds about right. What are you gonna do about it?"

She blushed harder even as she gave me a cute little glare. Then she inhaled slowly before her shoulders rolled back, and her eyes filled with deter-mination. I loved that she was trying so hard not to be shy and timid. But I also loved her sweet inno-cence. This girl...she was everything. Everything I could ever want and more than I could have ever imagined.

Somewhere in my mind, I'd already known I loved her, but I'd never admitted it, even to myself. I didn't know what it was about this particular moment—it seemed kind of an odd one for such a life altering revelation—but when an adorable little smirk graced her lips and her hands boldly gripped my vest, it hit me like a ton of bricks.

I'd already been obsessed with Blakely, obsessed with claiming her and owning her. But when the truth slammed into me, and I realized just how much I loved her, it only intensified every feeling. And fuck, I was gonna die if I didn't get inside her soon.

She pushed my vest off my shoulders, then slipped her hands beneath my T-shirt and pushed the material up. As my abs and chest were revealed, her eyes widened, and her mouth formed a little O.

I yanked the shirt over my head, then tossed it away before my hands went to the buttons of her shorts. But my movements stilled when I glanced at her face. Her eyes were roaming over every inch of my exposed skin, and I had to hold back a tortured groan when she licked her lips. My cock was so swollen that the zipper on my pants was digging into the shaft.

Then her gaze dropped to the very sizable bulge in my jeans, and she gasped. "Holy cow. You're... um...really...big."

The groan escaped, and I squeezed my eyes shut for a moment. "Baby, you can't say shit to me like that right now. I'm barely hanging on to my control."

"Oh, sorry."

I took both of her hands and laced our fingers together, squeezing them gently to gain her full attention. "You don't have to be sorry, baby. I don't ever want you to hold back from me. But this first time, I gotta be gentle. I don't want to hurt you any more than I have to."

She bit her lip nervously, once more looking at the evidence of my need for her. I raised her arms up and released her hands before encouraging her to lock them behind my neck. The position forced her to come closer until she was plastered up against my body.

"I'm not gonna lie, baby. I'm a big guy, and it's gonna be a tight fit. We'll go slow." I moved my hands up to cup her face and stared straight into her deep blue pools. "But I will be claiming you tonight, Blakely. Gonna pop your cherry, fill you with my come, and make you mine."

I didn't give her a chance to reply before sealing

my mouth over hers once more. Bending my legs a little, I grabbed her under her thighs and lifted her, then wrapped her legs around my waist. Carefully, I walked us in the direction of the bed. When I hit it, I bent forward so we fell onto the mattress.

She grumbled when I unlocked her legs from around my waist, and I chuckled. "Patience, baby."

Gliding my lips along her heated, silky skin, I moved down her body until I was kneeling at the edge of the bed. I unbuttoned her shorts and hooked my fingers into them, along with her underwear, and dragged them down and off her.

I gently pushed her legs open and shifted so I was between them, then froze. "Blakely, fuck," I gritted out through my clenched jaw. "You're fucking bare."

"Um...well..." Her cheeks turned deep red, and my rage built.

"Who did you do this for, Blakely?" I demanded. Whoever it was gonna die tonight.

"I...no one. I like the way it feels."

"Thank fuck." Relief surged through me, and hunger reignited the passion heating me from the inside out. "I love it, baby," I told her with a crooked smile. "Love that there is nothing between my mouth and my meal."

Blakely's skin flushed down to the dusky tips of her breasts, and I winked at her before settling her legs on my shoulders.

The smell of her sweetness mixed with her arousal had my cock nearly bursting, and I quickly unsnapped my jeans and freed it so I would have at least a little relief.

Using my thumbs, I parted her folds and groaned at the sight. "Fuck, baby. Look at this pretty pussy. Pink and swollen. And so fucking wet for me," I crooned as I swiped a finger down her center, then brought the digit to my lips to suck it clean. "It's all for me, right, Blakely?"

"Yes," she whispered.

"This is mine," I grunted before bending down and trailing the tip of my tongue lightly from bottom to top. "Who does it belong to, baby?"

"You," she panted, raising her hips in search of my touch.

"Only me," I growled as I slid my hands under her ass and brought her juicy center to my mouth. "Only ever me. No one else gets to be anywhere near my pussy."

"Gideon," Blakely gasped when I finally licked her with my flattened tongue before swirling the tip around her clit and going back down.

I fucking loved hearing her say my name in that breathy, hungry voice, but it was severely testing the limits of my control. I needed to make her come and get inside her before I lost it and blew my load all over the floor.

Using my tongue and teeth, I devoured her until her thighs quivered, and she cried out for completion. Then I slowly pushed a single finger into her channel and groaned at the snug fit. "So tight. Can't wait to feel you strangling my dick, baby." I raked my teeth over her hard bundle of nerves, causing a shiver to wrack her body. "But first, I want you to come on my tongue."

I withdrew the digit and thrust my stiffened tongue deep into her pussy just as I pinched her clit. Blakely's back arched, and she screamed my name as her juices flooded my mouth. I drank it greedily, then licked up any excess, determined to get every drop.

Knowing she'd be softer if she came again, I didn't give her a chance to recover before I drove her over the peak once more.

"Damn, you taste good. I think I could happily survive on just eating your pussy for the rest of my life."

Blakely giggled, and the sound sent something

warm trickling through my veins. "You'd starve," she teased.

I set her legs down and pushed to my feet, locking eyes with her and grinning. "Worth it."

She giggled again until her gaze dropped to my groin. My cock was long and thick, standing against my stomach with the head swollen and purple. "Um..."

"Relax, baby," I soothed while pushing my jeans and boxers down and stepping out of them. "Do you trust me?"

5

STORM

"Yes." Her immediate answer made me smile as warmth spread to my chest. "Then trust that I will take care of you."

She studied my hardness for another moment and licked her lips, making me groan silently at the thought of that little tongue stroking all over my shaft. Then looking back at my face, she scooted up to the center of the bed and lay back.

I grabbed one of her feet and kissed her ankle before continuing up her leg, leaving a trail of fiery kisses in my wake. At her belly button, I swirled my tongue around it, then continued upward to give each nipple a little bite. Blakely whimpered and tried to squeeze her legs together, but I was kneeling between them.

"Don't try to hide my pussy from me, Blakely," I admonished in a raspy voice. Gently, I widened her legs as far as they could comfortably go, then settled myself on top of her. I was so much larger than her that I covered her completely. My cock nestled in the apex of her thighs, baking in the heat radiating from her center. As I got into a comfortable position, each movement pushed my shaft into her, and her southern lips parted until they cradled me, bathing me in her juices.

Her tits pressed against my chest, the hard peaks scraping over my flesh with each of her heaving breaths. I grabbed her under her thighs and urged her to wrap them around my hips, then I captured both of her wrists in one of my hands and raised them up over her head.

Blakely's eyes widened, and she squirmed, trying to wiggle out of my grip, but I didn't budge. All she managed to do was rub herself against me, causing her to close her eyes and release a ragged moan.

"You said you trust me," I reminded her.

She opened her eyes, meeting my piercing stare as she nodded.

"Hold the headboard." I guided her hands up

and helped her wrap her fingers around the top of the bed, then kissed her softly. When she stayed in the position as I retreated, I smiled and praised, "Good girl."

Blakely's skin heated and flushed, but not from embarrassment. It was as if she'd been lit on fire.

Interesting.

"I love the way you say my name in that husky voice when you're aroused. It makes me want to worship your gorgeous body for hours."

Blakely's breath hitched, and she moaned, then bit her lip, cutting the sound off.

"Don't hold back, baby," I instructed firmly. "I want to hear your sounds of pleasure."

She nodded, and I gave her a soft kiss. "That's my girl."

"Gideon," she whimpered as her thighs squeezed my hips.

"You want my cock, Blakely?"

She nodded again, and I growled, "Tell me what you want, baby. Beg me to fuck you."

She groaned, and her pussy gushed with arousal, making it slick between us. Which would be a good thing when I entered her. "I want you," she choked out between choppy breaths.

I stayed still and waited until she let out a little

growl of frustration that had me forcing back a smile. How she could be so damn cute and sexy as hell all at once was beyond me.

"I want your...um...*cock*"—she whispered the last word, and I couldn't hold back my smile anymore—"inside me. Are you laughing at me?"

I shook my head and kissed her nose. "Absolutely not. I just think you're adorable, and it makes me smile."

Her brow furrowed, and she frowned. "Adorable?"

"And funny, smart, kind, and sexy as fuck."

"I am?" Her skin flushed once more, and I felt her heartbeat pick up.

Rocking my hips forward, I slid my thick rod through her drenched sex. "You feel that? How fucking hard I am?"

She jerked her chin up and down.

"That's all for you, baby. I own your addictive pussy, but my cock? He's all fucking yours."

"Gideon," she breathed, her legs tightening once more.

"Yeah, baby?"

"Take me. Make me yours."

More than ready, I slammed my mouth down on hers while twisting and plucking at her nipples as I moved my dick into position. The tip was just kissing the opening of her pussy, and already her heat was searing.

Breaking away from her, I stared deep into her blue pools as I slowly inched forward. With her arousal coating me, I slid in easily, but after just the tip was in, her inner walls clamped down.

I saw fucking stars, and my muscles clenched with the effort it was taking me to hold back my climax. "You feel so damn good, baby. You're gonna squeeze the fuck outta my cock."

Blakely moaned, and her fingers tightened around the headboard, turning her knuckles white.

"Good girl," I praised. Shifting my weight onto one elbow, I glided my other hand down her body and raised one leg up over my shoulder. Immediately, I sank a little farther, then I gently pushed in even more, going deeper inch by inch. I frequently stopped to let her adjust, giving her inner walls a chance to stretch to accommodate my massive girth.

Finally, I bumped against a barrier and was shocked by the strength of the wave of possession that flowed through me. Dropping my head, I took her mouth in a soul-deep kiss while I used one hand to rub her clit fast and hard. When she tore her mouth away and screamed in ecstasy, I slammed inside her, filling her until I was completely sheathed. "Mine." I grunted.

Blakely gasped, and I watched her face flash with pain. I was relieved when it was quickly overcome by the orgasm still rocking her body.

Unfortunately, the sensation of her inner walls rippling and clamping down on my shaft made it impossible for me to hold back. "Oh fuck," I groaned, dropping my head into the crook of her neck as my climax tore through me, and jets of hot come exploded from my dick.

It probably should have surprised me that when I finished coming, my cock was still rock hard. But I'd been dreaming of this moment for so long, and just the thought of my woman was enough to get me hard.

"Not done," I mumbled against her neck as I slowly withdrew and pushed back in until I was so deep, I bumped her cervix. "Still need to fuck you, baby."

"Yes," she gasped.

"It's gonna be fast and hard, Blakely," I warned her. Coming inside her hadn't helped me regain control. It had just fueled the primal need to mark her over and over. "Can you handle it? 'Cause this is your only chance to get me to back off."

"I'm tougher than I look," she murmured, and I couldn't help grinning.

"I'm well aware of how fucking awesome you are, baby. But I just popped your cherry, and you're already gonna be sore. If I fuck you like I want to now, you might not be able to walk for a week."

"Worth it," she whispered in my ear.

I lost my fucking mind, got up onto my knees, and put her other leg on my shoulder. I slammed inside her before pulling out almost all the way and doing it again. Then my animal instincts took over, and the only thing consuming my mind was hunger. Raw need had me rutting in her with desperation. "Fuck, Blakely," I grunted. "Oh, fuck yeah. That's it, baby. Your pussy takes my cock so good. Fuck!"

"Gideon!" Blakely cried out. "Please."

My eyes locked on her face when she begged, and she glanced upward.

"Touch me," I ordered.

Her expression flooded with happiness, and it ignited something else inside me, adding love to the passion, making her the center of my world.

Blakely's hands landed on my chest, then they were everywhere she could reach. Exploring every rigid muscle, tracing them and caressing, driving me wild.

"So tight," I grunted, pounding my shaft hard and deep, the tip smacking into her cervix with every thrust. After three orgasms, it was probably soft and open.

Oh shit. It suddenly hit me that I was fucking her bare. And had already come inside her once without protection.

"Are you on birth control?" I muttered, not slowing my thrusts in the least.

"Oh crap!" she exclaimed. "No! We should stop. We...oh, oh yes! Yes! Gideon! Harder!"

The second she told me she was unprotected and ripe, I knew I wasn't gonna stop until I'd filled her, stuffed her with my come and planted my kid in her belly. Rather than pulling back, I fucked her even deeper, slamming the headboard into the wall every time I drove my shaft into her tight channel.

"So good, baby. Love how tight you are. Fuck! Yes! Oh fuck, Blakely! Fuck!"

Blakely trembled, and her voice roughened as she shouted her pleasure. Begging for more and screaming my name. Her hands grabbed the sheets at her sides, and she clutched them, pulling hard as if they would keep her from flying away.

"Come, baby," I commanded. Grabbing her ankles, I pulled her legs down and draped them over my elbows, then widened my stance on my knees, keeping her spread as much as possible. When I bent slightly forward, the angle sent me plunging in even deeper, and my dick rubbed against her clit every time I went in or out.

"Gideon! Oh! Oh! Yes! Yes! Yesssss!"

She splintered apart, and her walls clamped around my cock, milking me and sucking me under. "Yes, baby! Fuck! Oh fuck!"

My spine tingled, and I dropped Blakely's legs, bending over her and supporting myself on my fists. I slammed into her one last time, as deep as I could possibly go. Then the dam burst inside me, and I bellowed as a tidal wave of heat and ecstasy rushed through my body. My cock erupted, flooding her womb with my seed, and every time I thought about it taking root, another stream of it would gush from my dick. It seemed like it might go one forever, but eventually, I emptied and collapsed on top of her, careful not to give her all of my weight.

"That was fucking amazing, baby," I mumbled as I rested my head between her tits.

"Incredible," she agreed breathily.

Her pulse was still frantic, and it made me smile, knowing she was just as affected by me as I was by her. I had to swallow back the impulse to tell her I loved her. It was too soon, and I wasn't sure she'd believe me if I said it for the first time right after sex.

Once I had enough strength to move, I crawled up her body and collapsed next to her, then pulled her into my arms. Her breathing evened out after a few minutes, and I wanted to fall asleep with her, but I didn't have long before I'd have to leave. Viper and I had shit to do, and I wanted to get it done ASAP so I could finally take my girl home.

6

BLAKELY

After everything that had happened with my foster family yesterday, the adrenaline rush from the orgasms Gideon had given me was enough to knock me out for about an hour. Waking up in his arms was even better than I imagined. If I had sat on Santa's lap this year, any Christmas wish I would have made wouldn't have compared to tonight's dream.

Not even in my wildest dreams did I ever think that Gideon had stayed away because he had feelings for me. The man was a negotiator who was known for his control, but he hadn't trusted himself not to act on his attraction before I turned eighteen. It was mind-blowing.

And so was the fact that I'd just given him my cherry.

"What're you thinking about?" Gideon brushed his lips against my ear as he rasped, "I can practically see the wheels turnin' in that sexy brain of yours."

Shifting in his arms so I could stare up at his gorgeous face, I smiled. "Just trying to wrap my head around what just happened."

His lips curved into a smirk. "You can do better than that, baby. Tell me what we just did, and I just might make you come again sooner than later."

"Ugh," I groaned, my cheeks heating as I buried my face in his broad chest. "It's one thing for me to talk dirty in the heat of the moment. It's a whole other thing when I'm not on the brink of an orgasm."

"Any time, day or night, it's sexy as fuck coming from your mouth." Pressing his finger under my chin, he tilted my head back until our gazes met again. "And I gotta admit I'm already addicted to your blushes. So don't be surprised if I want you to say as much dirty as fuck shit as I can get you to."

Winking at him, I murmured, "Then I guess you'll have to make it worth my while."

Rolling on top of me so that my back was pressed against the mattress and his dick was nestled between my thighs, he grinned down at me. "The three orgasms I gave you weren't enough to get you to talk about how my cock fucked you into a coma when I'm not still buried inside your sweet pussy?"

I quirked my brow as I playfully swatted at his chest. "Nope."

"Then I guess I'll just have to work on getting you used to telling me what you want when you're not come-drunk."

The way he phrased it made me think about something I didn't have the chance to do yet. I'd dreamed about having Gideon at my mercy while I had my lips wrapped around his dick...but that was before I had seen for myself what he was packing in his boxer briefs. Now I couldn't help but wonder if my mouth would even fit around his girth.

The heat in my cheeks deepened even more as I bit my bottom lip. There was a knowing gleam in Gideon's dark eyes as he tugged the flesh free with a smirk. "And I have a feeling it's not gonna take much to get you there, judging by the dirty thoughts I can see racing through your head."

"If you only knew," I teased, my tongue sweeping out to brush against his thumb.

"Hold that thought for when I can take you again without hurting you." His palm slid around to cup the back of my head as he bent low to claim my mouth in a deep kiss. "We gotta give your pussy a break. For a little while at least. I wasn't able to hold back as much as I wanted since it was your first time."

"Maybe you should've shown up sooner, like on my birthday. Then we would've been past me recovering from you popping my cherry, and we could be doing the things you want me to talk about."

My tone was teasing, but he must have heard the tiniest thread of doubt in my voice because his eyes turned serious. Rolling off me, he scooted up on the mattress so his back was resting against the headboard. Then he shifted me so I was cradled against his chest with his palm splayed against my lower back while I stared up at him. The steady beat of his heart in my ear while being wrapped in his embrace made me feel safe for the first time in so long.

"That was the plan, baby."

My eyes widened as I gasped, "It was?"

"I've been looking forward to coming for you on your eighteenth birthday for two years, Blakely." His hold on me tightened. "But my sister decided to show up a couple of weeks early to spend Christmas with me. Some bullshit about wanting to earn some money to cover expenses next semester instead of just letting me give her whatever she needs."

I had only met Elise a few times over the years, but I'd heard enough of Gideon's stories about his younger sister that I wasn't surprised she was being stubborn about wanting to cover some of her own expenses. Although he had left home when she was only eight, they were still close...and both could be obstinate when they had their minds set on something.

Besides Fox or Maverick, she was also one of the only people who could get Gideon to change his plans.

"I'm really glad you got to spend the holiday with your sister. How is she?"

A muscle jumped in his jaw as he growled, "Not good. Some bastard ran her off the road yesterday."

Pushing against his chest, I sat up and gawked at him. "What? Is she okay?"

"She's shaken up, but Blade looked her over and said her injuries were minor." He raked his fingers through his hair. "Cut her head and bruised her ankle."

"Did you catch the guy who did it?"

He shook his head. "Not yet, but the guys are on it. And they're keeping her safe at the clubhouse while I'm gone."

One of the things I loved most about Gideon was

his loyalty. He was so dedicated to the people he cared about, which had been a big part of why I'd been devastated when he dropped out of my life. Because it made me feel as though there was no chance that I was someone who was even a little important to him.

But knowing that he left with Elise's situation up in the air eased any fears I had about how much I meant to Gideon. He had trusted his club brothers to take care of her while he came for me himself. "Wow."

He reached out to stroke his thumb against my cheek, his fingers tugging on my jaw to pull my head down for a kiss. When his tongue tangled with mine, heat coursed through my veins. Clutching his shoulders, I pressed against him while he deepened the kiss. The chemistry between us exploded, and he rolled us until he hovered over me again.

Pressing his elbow into the mattress next to me, he lifted his other arm to cup my breast. I arched my back to press the pebbled peak deeper into his palm and moaned into his mouth. His dark eyes burned into mine as he broke off the kiss with a groan. "Fuck, baby. Not sure I can keep my cock outta you now that I finally have you right where you belong, beneath me."

I was a little achy between my legs, but that didn't stop me from wanting Gideon with a desperation that I didn't know was possible. "Then maybe you should stop trying and just take me again. Right here, right now."

"Or at least give you another—"

A loud knock on the door interrupted what he'd been in the middle of saying, and I pressed the back of my head against the pillows and cried, "Nooooo!"

A deep voice called, "C'mon, man. I hate to break this up, but I gave you as long as I could. We gotta roll now, or Fox is gonna have our heads when we get back."

"Fuuuuck," Gideon groaned, dropping his forehead against my breasts.

His breath was hot against my chest, which didn't do me any favors when it came to calming down. But I knew from his reaction that nothing else would happen until he took care of whatever the heck his club brother was talking about.

I might've only been twelve when my dad went to prison, but I still remembered how things worked in the MC world. If Gideon's president needed him to do something while he was in Florida, then he didn't have any choice but to leave. And if I wanted to be his old lady, I needed to show him that I understood what it took to stand by his side.

Pressing my lips against his cheek, I whispered, "Go take care of club business. I'll be here waiting for you when you're done."

7

STORM

I flicked down my kickstand and shut off my bike's engine, then swung my leg over the seat to dismount.

"Think you could stop your brooding long enough to get through this meeting?" Viper quipped, earning himself a dark scowl.

"I didn't think Storm had any other mood than brooding," said a deep, familiar voice.

Viper and I both looked at the warehouse door we'd parked in front of to see a tall, lean man in worn jeans and an old T-shirt that said, "If you're in control, you're not going fast enough."

He lounged against the entrance, his arms crossed over his chest and a smirk on his face. "Kane," I greeted my friend, lifting my chin.

Kane was big for a driver, but he was all toned muscle and stellar reflexes. His body knew exactly how to handle any race car he drove without having to think about it. Most people never guessed that he was a millionaire because they couldn't see beyond his shaggy hair, relaxed style, and easy smile. It was the same reason they never suspected that he was a merciless, lethal motherfucker. And he ran the underground racing world down here like the Mafia ran New York.

But he was as much my brother as Fox or any of the other Iron Rogues. He had helped me keep eyes and ears on Blakely over the years since I didn't fully trust her dad's MC.

"How was the reunion?" he asked, his smirk growing, making me want to break his jaw.

"You owe me a grand," Viper announced, and my gaze whipped around to see him grinning at Kane. "Told you she'd forgive him in less than a day."

Kane sighed and pushed away from the door, then shoved his hands in his pockets. "Can't believe you called it."

"We don't mess around when it comes to our women."

"Yeah, but I personally saw how pissed she was when someone mentioned him over the past two years. I really thought it would take him at least a week—"

"You were making bets on me and Blakely?" I snarled, interrupting their banter. There wasn't a lot of heat behind my irritation, though. It would have made me a fucking hypocrite, considering I'd been in on the betting pools when my other brothers had been going after their old ladies.

Kane shrugged and turned around, walking inside the building without another word. This wasn't unusual behavior for him. When he was done with something, he moved on, and you either went with or were left behind. I couldn't fucking wait for the day when he met his woman because the right one was gonna knock him on his ass.

Viper and I followed Kane, walking into the offices that looked out over an extremely large garage where his employees were working on multiple race cars. We ascended a set of stairs that led us to Kane's office. He walked around his desk and stood facing the window that took up almost the entirety of the back wall. It gave him a view of the entire track below and most of the stadium seating.

"You bring it?" he asked as he pivoted and settled his piercing stare on me, his expression sober.

I pulled a folded sheet of paper from the pocket

of my cut and held it up with two fingers before placing it on the desktop.

Kane nodded. "I owe you."

"Bullshit," I grunted.

A year ago, Kane had discovered that someone was pushing drugs at his races. Like my MC, he did his best to keep that shit away from his establishments, but it was impossible to keep them out completely, considering the crowds that attended the events. But this time, it was a date rape drug, and he had zero tolerance for that shit.

He'd immediately called Fox, and we'd all been working hard to identify the supplier. But the dealers were too fucking scared of him to talk. Deviant had written a program to go through all of the security footage for the races and detect certain situations that might be a handoff. However, between the Iron Rogues and Kane's organization, plus the places we owned together, it was a fuck ton of video to get through.

A few times, he caught a buy but wasn't able to identify the players because of angles or crowd obstructions or whatever. Then last week, he finally got us an ID. It was a low-level pusher, but he'd been stupid enough to lead us to his dealer, who led us to the next in the chain, and on and on until we finally found the source.

He was also a rival bookie and rumored to cheat his customers and then hurt their loved ones as "punishment" for crossing him.

Fox sent me and Viper to aid the team Kane put together to go after this guy. We were both former military special forces, and since it was my hometown, I'd be able to come for Blakely. She still had a semester of school left, but I wasn't waiting any longer, so I had irons in the fire to take care of that situation too.

Now, my plans included one more thing before I could take my woman home.

"You don't owe me for helping to wipe out an evil son of a bitch. We're fucking brothers, Kane. I always have your back. But I could use your help with something."

Kane pulled out his chair and sat down. "Go on."

I filled him in on the situation with Blakely's foster brother and parents. When I finished, he still looked relaxed and at ease, like always. But I'd known him long enough to see the slight hardening of his jaw and the ice chips in his eyes.

"You have a plan?" he asked.

I nodded and told him what I'd come up with.

He made a couple of suggestions that were devious as hell and a little bit twisted, which was why I'd asked his advice.

"After we handle Comdon, give me twenty-four hours to get everything in place."

"Done," I replied. "Thanks, man."

"Don't thank me," he muttered, raising an eyebrow as his piercing gaze drilled into me. "We're brothers. I always have your back."

"Enough of this mushy shit," Viper snarked. "My trigger finger is getting itchy."

I rolled my eyes and reached out to slap the back of his head. "You know where the armory is. Get ready to head out."

"Tatum should already be there," Kane said, referring to his number two. He was also his younger brother and an arms specialist. Not to mention a world class race car driver.

Tatum had a laid-back attitude and quick smile that hid the fact that he was a little bit psycho, which came in handy when someone needed torturing...or when he was racing.

"New shit arrived this morning," Kane continued. "Since then, he's been locked away playing with his toys."

Viper grinned and spun on his heel, leaving without a comment or backward glance.

———

Kane pointed at the gate at the back of the property, and I nodded. I looked at Viper and gestured for him to go. He slinked out of the tree line and approached the cinder block wall, coming to a stop just out of sight.

The property was several acres, but Comdon had every entrance and exit patrolled. The wall surrounding the house was at least seven feet tall, and it would have been a decent defense if it didn't have four gates and trees just outside that were high enough for a sniper perch.

Kane's men had scouted the area earlier and reported seeing a fucking army of guards. Comdon was obviously paranoid. Rightly so.

Viper knelt on the ground and set down the duffel he was carrying. After opening it, he dug around until he found the right items. Among Viper's many skills, he was extremely talented in the demolition department. He and Tatum had cooked up a couple of explosives to blow the gate without making a huge ruckus. The charges would blow the hinges, but the explosion would be relatively quiet.

I met Kane's gaze again and jerked my chin toward one of the trees. He signaled to Tatum, who grinned and immediately climbed the tree, somehow doing it without a sound. After settling, he lifted the rifle slung around his back and checked the scope. Then he found a comfortable perch and tapped his thigh twice with two fingers.

A shadow passed by the gate, and Kane glanced at his watch before tapping his thigh twice. Tatum's shoulders moved as he exhaled slowly, and then his finger twitched on the trigger.

The shadow behind the gate hit the ground, and I drew a circle above my head to signal Viper. We had less than five minutes before one of the other guards would radio the dead guy to check in.

Viper stepped out of the shadows and quickly placed his charges, then grabbed his bag and jogged back over to our hiding spot. His thumb pressed on the screen of his phone, and there was a *pop pop pop pop* before the gate wobbled and fell.

One of Kane's guys ran over and retrieved the radio from the fallen guard. It crackled, and someone spoke in Spanish. Our guy replied in a low, bored grumble so his voice wouldn't be recognized.

Kane motioned for us to step close, then he whispered, "Shoot to kill. I don't want a single one of these fuckers feeding their shit to anyone ever again."

Each of us nodded, then proceeded with the plan we'd devised.

It took less than ten minutes for Viper, Kane, Tatum, and I to get into the house. I didn't know where Comdon had hired his security from, but they were useless. I even managed to sneak all the way up to one and snap his neck.

Tatum rolled his eyes and muttered, "Serves him right for being such a dumb fuck."

When we walked into the house, we split into twos, and while the brothers went up the stairs to search the second floor, Viper and I made our way through the bottom. We didn't find anyone until we reached the kitchen. There were two security guys and three people huddled around a small table.

I caught Viper's eye and tilted my head back toward the hallway. He backed up into the shadows while I plastered myself next to the doorway. A loud crash came from Viper's direction, and just as I'd assumed would happen, the two henchmen came rushing out to see what was going on. Almost simultaneously, they dropped silently to the ground, one with a bullet in the back of his skull and the other with a hole right between the eyes.

The woman and two men at the table were standing when I peeked back into the room. I expected them to look nervous or on guard, but with one glance at their faces, I realized they were all blitzed.

Sighing, I stepped fully into the kitchen and shot the two men in quick succession. Then I hesitated because it went against my nature to harm a woman. "I don't want to kill you," I informed her quietly. "But I will if you make one sound."

She nodded, but the movement must have messed with her equilibrium because she swayed and passed out, crumpling to the floor.

"Fucking hell," I muttered.

"You've got quite a way with the ladies," Kane grunted from right behind me.

I glanced over my shoulder and raised an eyebrow.

"It's done," he said, answering my unspoken question.

"What do you want to do with her?" Viper asked as he strolled into the room.

"I recognize her from Deviant's research," I murmured. "She's his current fuck buddy. Spent three years in prison for drug possession and has only been out for six months. Drop her at the nearest police station"—I gestured to the drug paraphernalia on the table that was clearly packaged for selling— "with some of that shit on her and she'll be charged with a first-degree felony and get at least ten years. Plus whatever they give her for breaking parole."

Tatum had joined us by the time I finished, and he scratched his chin as he spoke in a thoughtful tone. "I can get in touch with Flemming and make sure the charges stick."

"Detective on our payroll," Kane explained.

"Other option is to take her with us and see what she knows," Torin, one of Kane's right-hand men, suggested. "Comdon answered to someone."

Kane's gaze fell on me for a moment before he answered. "Take her to the cabin and let her dry out while I handle something else for the next couple of days."

I nodded my thanks since I knew he was putting off the interrogation to help me.

"I'll call in the cleaners." Tatum pressed on the screen of his phone, then put it to his ear. "Clean up on aisle five," he said before hanging up.

Kane rolled his eyes and swirled his finger in the air. "Move out."

When we arrived back at Kane's building, Viper and I stayed on our bikes. I was more than ready to get back to my girl.

"Shouldn't need more than twenty-four hours," Kane told me, standing next to my motorcycle with his arms crossed over his chest. "But we got some of what we needed at the house, so it might be less."

"Thanks, man," I replied. We shook hands, then he lifted his chin in farewell before pivoting and stalking to the entrance of his warehouse.

It was late when we arrived back at the clubhouse, and I didn't want to wake Blakely, especially since she'd need her energy for what I had planned when she woke up. So I stripped out of my clothes and crawled into the bed, then pulled her into my arms. Taking a deep breath, I filled my lungs with her cinnamon scent and fell into a contented sleep.

8

BLAKELY

Waking up in Gideon's arms was everything I ever wanted, and I enjoyed every minute of it, even though he'd been sound asleep. I wasn't sure how late he'd been out, but he barely moved when I finally slid off the mattress to use the bathroom. I used his exhaustion to my advantage and slipped on some clothes before quietly padding out of the room to head down to the kitchen. Assuming that my man would be hungry when he woke up, I wanted to bring him breakfast in bed.

I wasn't surprised to find Staci standing at the stove since she loved to cook. Flashing me a smile over her shoulder, she greeted, "Morning."

"Good morning," I murmured.

She wagged her brows. "Have a good night?"

Blushing, I nodded. "Yeah, the best."

"Mmmhmm, I'm sure you did." After lowering the heat on the burner she was using to cook French toast, she turned toward me. "I hope you know what you're doing with Storm because your dad is going to flip out when he finds out about you two. As far as he's concerned, you're still his baby girl, especially since he hasn't been able to really see you grow up."

I knew my dad couldn't do much to Gideon from jail—especially since he was an Iron Rogue and going up against them would put the men in his club at risk. But my dad's reaction to me being with the man he'd trusted to look out for me all these years freaked me out. Hoping for more time before word got back to him, I downplayed what was going on. "I think it's way too soon to worry about what my dad might think about Gideon and I being together. It's only been a day."

Staci's gaze darted over my shoulder, and her eyes widened. That was all the warning I got before Gideon's arms wrapped around me as he growled, "Guess I gotta show you what a difference one day can make to your life. 'Cause no way in hell am I taking a step back after last night. Not for anyone, even your dad."

Then he threw me over his shoulder as though it

was nothing, and I squealed, kicking my feet, even though I loved how easily he carried me. "Gideon, what are you doing?"

"You heard me,'" he grunted, taking the steps two at a time, still lifting me like I was lighter than air. "Gotta show my woman what last night meant."

The steely determination in his voice sent a delicious shiver down my spine. Gideon was the only man who I had ever been interested in. His reaction to an offhand comment made me feel so desired. And not just because he'd already taken me to bed.

Throwing open the door, he didn't even break his stride as he shut it behind us and then plopped me down on the mattress. Crouching so we were at eye level, those gorgeous dark brown eyes met mine, full of fire and something else that already had my panties damp.

"What did you mean by it only being a day?" he growled.

I shrugged, feeling my cheeks becoming overpoweringly hot. "That we've only been together a day, you know..."

He gripped my chin with his fingers. "I don't know, baby. But what I do know is that you're mine, and I'm yours. Do you understand that? I don't just fuck to fuck. Before I even took your sweet cherry, it was all over for me. I knew back when you were too young for me to touch that we were going to belong to each other, and what happened between us in this bed yesterday just confirmed it."

He'd already said something similar last night, but hearing it again struck me even more. His fingers trailed down my arms, leaving goose bumps in their wake.

"You really knew?" I asked, my voice coming out a whisper.

"Yes. And you understand that you're mine?" he asked.

I swallowed hard and nodded, my voice getting caught in my throat.

"Good girl," he growled before crushing his lips to mine and taking my breath away.

His hands tangled in my hair as he pressed my body flat against the mattress. Then his full lips skimmed along the neckline of my shirt, scratching me with his beard, but I didn't mind. All I could focus on was the immense pleasure already building between my thighs.

"It hasn't even been a day, but it feels like this greedy pussy needs some attention," he murmured, rubbing his hand over my jeans.

The exquisite friction was almost too much as I

moaned, bucking my hips to meet his hand. "Yes, please."

He laughed against my sensitive skin. "Then be my good girl and tell me what you want."

With expert stealth, my jeans and panties were off, exposing my bare pussy to his waiting hands. "You," I gasped. "I need to feel you inside me again. Please."

His mouth was back on mine as he parted my folds, skimming his fingers over my arousal. "So wet for me already, baby. It only took a day for your sweet pussy to become addicted to my cock, didn't it?"

"It did."

I had a feeling I wasn't going to live down that comment for a long while. But if he gave me a little sexual torture, followed by orgasms, when he brought it up...who was I to argue?

"Good, because I'm fucking obsessed with your pussy, baby." He pulled back, putting his wet finger to my lips. "See, taste yourself."

I slowly licked his finger, tasting the salty sweetness.

"That's so fucking hot, baby. Now I gotta taste your sweet pussy too."

"Please," I murmured, my inner walls fluttering.

"Good girl." Crawling down my body, he smirked.

"Spread wide for me, baby. I need full access to this perfect pussy that's all mine." He pressed his palms against my thighs, pushing me open for his mouth.

Keeping his heated gaze on mine, he licked a slow, long stroke up my center, my thighs already shivering around him.

"Is my pussy too sore for me to stretch you out with my big fingers?" he murmured into my folds.

"No, stretch me, please."

He hooked a finger inside me, and my hips immediately jumped off the bed. Then his expert finger hit a spot that had stars sparking behind my eyelids.

"Look at me while I taste you, Blakely. I want you to watch as you come on my tongue."

I forced my eyes open, meeting his hooded stare as he lapped me up like I was the most delicious lollipop he'd ever had. Gripping the sheets, I tried to stay still, but my thighs shook as I bucked my hips forward to meet his awaiting lips. He growled in pleasure, adding another finger as he circled his lips around my clit, breaking down all of my walls as I crashed down.

My orgasm hit hard and fast as I rode my release against his face.

But he didn't stop. Even with my arousal dripping down his beard, he lapped me all up and used his fingers faster, bringing me to another orgasm. This time, the pleasure was so intense that my eyelids drifted close as my entire body shook, moaning loudly as I called his name again and again. "Gideon! Oh yes! Yessss!"

"That's it, baby. Come for me so your tight little pussy will be ready to take my big, fat cock again," he growled, moving his mouth back to my lips.

His kiss was deep and full of passion. Want.

I couldn't get his clothes off fast enough, pawing at his shirt and vest. He laughed against my skin, pulling back to toss aside his clothes and then rip what remained of mine off me.

He didn't say anything, just leaned over, taking one of my nipples in his mouth as his hands went back to my wet and wanting sex.

"Please, fuck me, Gideon. Please."

He looked up at me with a spark in his dark eyes. "That's my good girl, asking for exactly what she wants."

Kneeling between my legs, I could already make out the precome on his massive length before he slid slowly into my wetness inch by exquisite inch. He stayed balls deep inside for a moment, letting my body adjust to the fullness.

"Fuck, baby, your tight little pussy feels so good against my cock. Squeeze it for me. Show me how you want me to fuck you."

I pushed my hips to his, soft at first, then harder, feeling him hit all the way to my womb.

"Such a good girl," he murmured, gripping my waist as he met my thrust, my knees quaking as another orgasm already built in my sensitive body.

"I'm going to come again," I panted, clawing at his chest and gripping his biceps.

"That's it, baby. Come for me. Coat my cock. Let me feel it all around me."

He pounded harder, his hand going between us to circle my clit with his thumb as he matched my thrusts.

My entire body shook as my climax ripped through me, and I gripped him hard as I rode out the wave. "Gideon!"

"That's right, baby. My name is the only one those perfect lips of yours are ever gonna say when you're coming. Because you're all mine."

"Yes, I'm yours," I whimpered.

"Can't wait to come in this pussy again, baby. Want me to fill you up?"

"Yes, please," I managed to breathe.

He moaned, thrusting a few more times before he filled me completely, another orgasm hitting me at the same time as everything went dark around me, sparks shooting through my toes and back up through my stomach.

I leaned back on the pillows, trying to catch my breath as my eyelids fluttered open to meet Gideon's smile. "I don't think I can move."

He laughed, slowly getting up and going into the bathroom.

He returned with a damp washcloth, cleaning up between my thighs before tossing it aside. My stomach chose that moment to let out a loud growl, making him chuckle. "Guess now that I've made my point, it's past time to feed my woman."

My plans to make him breakfast in bed had gone out the window, but I had zero complaints after the orgasms I'd gotten instead.

9
———————

STORM

My phone vibrated against my chest, and I pulled it from the inside pocket of my cut. When I saw Kane flashing on the screen, I kissed Blakely's temple and told her I'd be right back.

It had been less than a day, so I was surprised to hear from him so soon.

"Kane," I answered once I'd stepped into the hallway.

"We got seriously fucking lucky. You need to head out now."

"Where?"

"At their fucking house." Kane sounded almost gleeful. Well, as much as a guy like Kane could.

"I'll be there in twenty."

I shoved my phone in my pocket and walked

back over to where Blakely sat on a stool at the bar, chatting with a couple of old ladies.

"Baby." I turned the stool so she was facing me, and when she smiled, my heart skipped a beat. "Gotta go for a bit."

"I'll come with you," she chirped. But I grabbed her waist to keep her still before she could jump down off the stool.

"Need you to stay here where I know you're safe. Viper is gonna be here with you."

Blakely's pretty mouth turned down into a frown. "Are you going to do something dangerous?"

I didn't want her to even think about those people any more, even if it was to know their lives would be miserable from this day forward. So I put it in the "club business" category and evaded her question. "Just doing a favor for a friend."

"That didn't answer my question, Storm," she snapped.

My eyes narrowed, and my grip on her tightened. I was about to correct her but stopped when a thought hit me, and I smiled instead. She huffed at my expression, but I wasn't about to tell her my discovery. If she always called me Storm when she was irritated or pissed at me, it gave me an edge. And

I knew she was gonna be a handful, so I'd take any advantage I could get.

"You're right. It didn't. But you grew up in this life, baby. You know there are always going to be some things I can't tell you."

Her muscles relaxed a little, and she nodded. "Yeah. I do know that. I just...I just want you to be safe."

I cupped her face and spoke in a solemn tone. "There is no way in hell that I will let anything take me away from you, Blakely."

She stared into my eyes for a few moments, then sighed. "Okay. But I reserve the right to kick your butt if you get hurt."

I tossed my head back and let out a deep laugh. "Fuck, you're adorable." She huffed, and I gave her a quick kiss. "You can try."

I kissed her again, then jogged up to our room to grab my keys and wallet. She and Viper were both standing by the door when I came down. He jerked his head toward the exit, then walked out, leaving me relatively alone with Blakely. I yanked her into my arms and kissed the fuck out of her. "Hopefully, I'll only be gone for a couple of hours."

"Okay," she whispered, still looking a little

dazed. I turned her around and patted her ass to get her going, then walked out into the parking lot.

"Kane called?" he asked.

"Apparently, shit is happening now. I need you to stay with Blakely in case things go sideways."

"And because you don't like her being here alone with the men."

I shrugged unrepentantly. "That too."

He grinned and shook his head. "Going soft, just like Prez."

I scoffed as I climbed onto my bike. "First of all, say that again in front of him. But make sure I'm there to watch him kick your ass. Or put a bullet in your head. Second, love doesn't make you soft. It makes you whole, which means you're stronger."

Viper snorted and turned around to walk back to the door. "I'll take your word for it. I'd rather not test that theory on myself."

Smiling, I started my bike and pulled out of the parking lot. The day Viper met his woman would be real fucking interesting. I looked forward to saying, "I told you so."

Kane and Tatum were waiting for me a couple of blocks down from the home of Blakely's former foster parents. When I pulled up beside them and cut the engine, Kane didn't waste time filling me in.

"We planted the drugs this morning, and I had a guy on the little shit to make sure he didn't surprise us."

"He surprised us alright," Tatum drawled, his mouth curved into a smirk.

"What?" I was confused.

Kane tossed Tatum a dark look that told him to shut the hell up before he continued. "After what happened with Blakely, I had a feeling that wasn't the first time he'd gone after a younger woman, but it wasn't something we could prove without more time and surveillance."

"I had the same thought," I agreed. Which was why we'd decided to go with planting drugs and had paid a local dealer to finger Bryan as his supplier.

"Torin contacted me right before I called you. Seems Bryan couldn't keep it in his pants any longer."

As disgusted as I was, I had a feeling where Kane was going with this and it definitely lightened my mood.

"She's under eighteen, isn't she?" Since Bryan

was twenty-four, if she was under age, he could spend up to fifteen years in prison. And with the drugs...I doubted he'd be out any time soon. Assuming that Blakely's dad didn't shank him in prison.

"Yup," Tatum crowed. His smile would look easy to most anyone, but I knew him well enough to see the hint of disgust. If this was his plan, Bryan and his parents would both end up in the mouth of a croc-odile. But I wanted them to suffer like they'd made Blakely suffer. To live a miserable life, outcast by the people who were supposed to be there for them and treated like they were beneath everyone around them. "Best part is that they are fucking in Mommy and Daddy's bed."

"No," disagreed Kane. "The best part is that Mommy and Daddy are at a church meeting."

Apparently, I'd done something right in this life because things couldn't have been planned any better.

Blakely's foster parents were heavily involved in their church, and the majority of the congrega-tion was just like them. Shallow, two-faced hypocrites.

And the church only a block in the other direction from their house. This meant that when the police arrived, they'd all come running to see what the fuss was about.

"What did you do to get the police at his door?" I queried.

"We tipped off the girl's parents," Tatum replied. Then he smirked. "Did I forget to mention that they also belong to their church?"

I'm gonna need some fucking popcorn for this shit.

I LEANED against a lamp post across the street from the Davidson's house and snickered at the comical sight. If Patti had been wearing pearls, she would have been clutching them dramatically. She was crying as she stared at the police escorting Bryan—who was half dressed—out of the house in cuffs. But I didn't miss the covert glances she tossed around, cringing when she saw all the people gathered around.

One of her church friends was patting her back, all the while staring at the spectacle with wide eyes like it was her favorite daytime soap opera. Not that it was a far-fetched comparison.

As expected, several other members of the

congregation had come outside when they heard the sirens. Word must have spread quickly because there was quite the crowd witnessing Patti's fall from grace.

A very young woman was also guided out of the house, and for a moment, she looked shocked when she saw the crowd. Then her face crumpled melodramatically, and she burst into tears as she ran over to an older couple and threw herself into the man's arms.

I was a little surprised to see Scott standing stoically beside his wife, showing no emotion whatsoever. It made me wonder if he'd been expecting this to happen someday.

"Think the dad knew about his son's proclivity for fucking underage women?" Kane asked, voicing my thoughts out loud.

"Not sure. But he certainly didn't stand up for Blakely when his son tried to take advantage of her and his wife threw her out. If he knew about Bryan's depravity and did nothing, that makes him just as much of an asshole as his son."

The crowd parted to make a path for the police officers to get to their car, but they kept their eyes on the house because another officer exited the front door holding an evidence bag. "Found this in the dresser drawer."

I wasn't sure what drew Patti's attention, but she suddenly looked my way.

Her eyes grew big and round when she spotted me. I nodded my head, both in a mocking greeting and a confirmation that I was behind this.

After a second, she sprang to life and ran up to one of the officers. She gestured in my direction, and I could see that she was speaking rapidly. The officer listened for a second, then rolled his eyes and said something to her that made her snap her mouth shut and back up.

When she whipped her gaze to me again, I smirked. The cop wasn't even on our payroll and he'd done exactly what one of our guys would have done.

"It was him!" she abruptly shouted, pointing at me. "He set up my poor son!"

The same police officer she'd spoken to sighed in annoyance, while his partner—who *was* on our payroll—glanced over to see who she was referring to.

I put a confused expression on my face and put my hands out to my sides, then shrugged.

"My son wouldn't have done this if he hadn't been tricked!"

"We could have sold tickets to this circus," Tatum murmured, making me chuckle.

"Ma'am," the officer sighed. "You can't just go around accusing people on the street for no reason," he said loudly enough for it to be heard by everyone.

"My daughter was the one who was tricked!" The man holding the sobbing young woman yelled. "And we'll be pressing charges."

Patti gasped and turned to her husband, speaking furiously in a low voice. He shrugged after a second, then turned and went into the house.

The expressions of the crowd slowly shifted to haughty disgust, and when the cruiser drove away, they quickly dissipated, leaving Patti standing all alone. She looked scared and utterly defeated.

"We're done here," I announced as I climbed onto my bike.

"Wait," Tatum muttered, grabbing my biceps.

He was peering at the house, and I turned my head to see what had caused him to stop me from leaving. Scott stood on the porch with a duffel bag in one hand as he slipped a pair of sunglasses on his face. He spoke to Patti, whose face drained of color, then stalked off the porch and over to a sensible white sedan.

"Cherry on top," Tatum snickered.

"What are you going to do about him?" Kane asked, well aware that I wouldn't let this go until all three of their lives were ruined.

"He works for the church," I informed them. "There's no way he'll keep his job, and he certainly won't get a reference. Also, Deviant hacked his credit and trashed it. He won't be able to rent anywhere. So he'll have to live in shitty motels until the money runs out, then go crawling back to his wife. Who will never let him forget he abandoned her."

"Can't think of a worse punishment than being stuck with that bitch for the rest of my life," Tatum commented with a grimace.

I nodded and met Kane's piercing stare. "That other thing?" I asked.

He nodded. "He'll be sent to Saber's cell block after he's arraigned. He'll be waiting for the mother-fucker." His lips tipped up in a rare smile. "And you know what they'll do to someone like him."

I was counting on it. Criminals or not, a lot of prisoners had no tolerance for anyone who was being charged with a sexual crime. Especially involving someone underage. Bryan would be breathing through a tube before long...if he even survived. But Saber would be out, so there'd be no blowback that would keep him from Blakely.

"Thanks," I muttered gruffly, and the brothers both jerked their chins up in acknowledgment.

"Tell Fox I have a new guy racing next month. He should come down and check him out."

"Will do."

As I pulled out onto the road, I felt lighter now that all that shit was dealt with. My focus was all on Blakely and our future.

10

BLAKELY

"Your man will be here any minute," Viper muttered.

He'd said maybe a dozen words in the hours since Gideon had left, but I didn't take offense. I just assumed that he was the silent type, like so many of the bikers I'd met when I was growing up.

I heaved a deep sigh of relief at knowing he was okay. Him leaving his club brother behind to watch over me was unsettling. It made me worry that whatever he did was much more dangerous than the club business they'd handled yesterday. I wished he'd taken Viper with him to watch his back. "Thanks."

He gave me a chin lift in response, then lifted his bottle of beer to his lips.

Sliding off the stool I'd been sitting on, I waved

off his concern when he moved to follow me. "Don't worry. I'm not going far. Just going to wait for Gideon near the front door."

"Good call." He set the bottle back down with a nod. "Storm's got something he's gonna want to share with you."

My brows went up at his reply...and not just because it was more words than I'd heard him string together before. I hadn't expected Gideon to tell me what he'd been doing since he had said it was club business. I had taken that explanation at face value without wondering much about where he had gone because I assumed I would never know. But now my curiosity got the better of me, and I twisted my hands together while I heard the unmistakable rumble of bikes pulling up in front of the clubhouse.

As soon as Gideon walked through the door, I threw myself in his arms. It was almost impossible to believe how much my life had changed in only a few short days. I wasn't sure when or if I would ever see him again, and now his club brother was calling him "my man."

"You're back," I whispered.

"Yup." He wrapped my hair around his fist and tugged my head back to claim my mouth in a deep kiss. "And I have some damn good news for you, baby."

"You do?" I asked.

Pulling his phone from the back pocket of his jeans, he tapped on the screen to pull up a story on the web browser. Then he tilted the screen toward me so I could read it. As I scanned the headline, my eyes went wide. "Holy crap! Bryan was arrested?"

"Damn fucking straight," Gideon confirmed. "And it couldn't have happened to a better guy."

Reading the story, I gasped. "For statutory rape and drugs?"

"Yup, and the drug charges are gonna be a felony since they got him on possession with the intent to distribute. He's going away for a long time."

The first charge was easy to believe after what he'd tried to pull with me, but he'd never struck me as a drug dealer. With the money his parents gave him, I couldn't understand why he would take a risk like that. "Wow."

"The bastard should've known better than to fuck with you."

There was a thread of satisfaction in his voice that made me wonder if he'd been behind Bryan's arrest, but I decided it was better not to ask after he'd called it club business.

Twining my arms around his neck, I went on my toes to brush a kiss against his cheek. "I'm safe now and never have to worry about him or his parents again."

"Now that they're taken care of, we can talk about what all we need to do for the move up to Old Bridge. I shoulda thought about bringing a prospect up to drive your truck back so you could ride on the back of my bike. Maybe Jagger will lend me a guy. He can rent a car or fly back down here."

"Whoa, hold up." I dropped my arms to press my palms against his broad chest. "I can't just move to Tennessee all of a sudden."

His fingers clenched my waist, his eyes narrowing as he stared down at me. "I get that this is moving quickly, but I waited two long years for you, baby. Not gonna have a long-distance relationship, and I can't stay with the Westland Riders MC. I have responsibilities to my own club, and you belong with me."

"I'm not arguing about any of that." I heaved a deep sigh. "I guess I was so wrapped up in finally getting everything that I dreamed of that I didn't stop to think about how the logistics would work."

"That's what you've got me around for," he

boasted with a cocky grin. "You tell me what you need, and I make it happen."

His offer was sweet, but I didn't think my problem had an easy fix. "I still have one more semester to go before I graduate, and it starts next week. I can't just leave, not without transferring to another school, which would totally suck since I wouldn't know anyone there. Not that I have a ton of close friends here when I never felt comfortable inviting anyone to my home."

"I'm fucking sorry I didn't know how bad things had gotten for you." The regret was clear in his dark eyes as he added, "I had people watching over you, but it wasn't enough. I shoulda manned up and played a more active role in your life while I waited for when I could finally claim you. I hate that my inability to trust my self-control around you ended up with you being hurt."

"Stop," I whispered, pulling on his arm to lead him upstairs. Our conversation was getting heavier than I expected, and I didn't want to have it where someone could overhear. When we were behind the closed door, I gestured toward the chair and then climbed on his lap after he sat down. "As much as I wish we would've been able to spend time together over the past two years, I also kind of love that your feelings for me are so strong that you didn't think you could be around me without acting on them. It makes me feel...powerful."

"Because you are, baby." His palm stroked up and down my spine, sending goose bumps in its wake. "I hate to clue you in, but nobody in the world has the kind of influence over me that you do."

I'd kind of assumed that he acted differently with me than anyone else, but I loved how he straight up admitted it to me. Grinning at him, I murmured, "I promise to use my powers for good, if that makes you feel any better. And orgasms. Lots and lots of them."

"As many as you want," he vowed, his eyes getting darker with desire. "But first we gotta figure out what it's gonna take for you to come back to Tennessee with me because I'm not leaving Florida without you."

Wincing, I murmured, "I really don't want to be a high school dropout, but maybe I could get my GED or something?"

"Or I could pull some strings to get your school to agree for you to finish off your last few classes online instead of having to show up in class," he suggested.

My brows arched as I tilted my head to the side. "Is that even possible?"

"Sure as fuck is." He flashed me a cocky smirk that made my panties wet. "Never would've thought of it except I've heard stories about a couple of the guys in the Silver Saints MC managing to swing it when they fell for women who hadn't graduated yet. So I already put some feelers out."

"You did?" I gasped.

"Not sure why you're so surprised, baby. I knew that when I came for you, I was gonna take you back with me. Figured the school thing would need to be figured out and didn't want to leave it till the last minute."

Each time I got more proof of the thought he'd put into coming down here for me, it bolstered my confidence. "Then I guess I'll leave it in your more than capable hands."

"I got it covered, baby." He brushed his lips against mine. "Things are coming together with the school, so you don't need to worry about anything other than figuring out what you want to take with us."

I needed to do one other thing if I was going to move to Tennessee with Gideon. "I need to see my dad before we leave."

11

STORM

"I'm nervous," Blakely whispered, her grip on my hand tightening.

"Relax, baby. It's not like you haven't been in contact with your dad," I reminded her as I handed my ID to the clerk. It had taken a few days to get in to see him, and it'd been just long enough for her to build up this conversation in her mind.

"Yeah, but...I mean, I know it's you, but you're still a guy."

The clerk made a little sound when she took Blakely's license, and I glanced at the woman to see her eyes doing an appreciative sweep of my body.

I frowned and opened my mouth, but Blakely distracted me when she cuddled into my side and glared daggers at the woman. "*My* guy," she snapped.

My mouth spread into a grin, and I captured her chin with two fingers and turned her face up to mine. "Too fucking right." Then I sent my own scowl at the woman behind the glass, who immediately averted her eyes.

A buzzer filled the air, and the door to the visitor's area of the prison swung open. As we walked through, I bent my head to whisper in Blakely's ear. "Do you have any idea how damn sexy it is when you get territorial over me? Makes me hard as fuck."

She shivered but glared up at me adorably. "You can't talk to me like that right before we see my dad!" she whispered.

I laughed. "It's not like he can hear me, baby."

"Yeah, but you get this smoldering look..." Her cheeks turned pink as she trailed off, and I couldn't help laughing once more.

"Storm?"

Blakely and I both turned to find her dad standing at the entrance to the room, staring at me incredulously.

"Did you just laugh? I don't think I've ever even seen you smile..."

I shrugged. "You've never seen me with Blakely."

"Hi, Daddy," she greeted him softly.

He lost interest in me immediately and smiled widely at his daughter. "Hey there, pretty girl." His gaze swept over Blakely, and he blinked a few times, but not before I saw the way his eyes shined with a little moisture. "You look amazing. All grown up."

Blakely had only been allowed to visit him when I came and brought her to the prison, so she hadn't seen him often, and not for the past couple of years. Another thing I needed to make up to her.

He moved to a table and gestured for her to sit before taking his own seat. I pulled out a chair for Blakely, then sat in the one next to her and threw my arm over the back of hers.

Saber frowned at my arm, but Blakely asked him a question, and he focused on chatting with her.

Finally, I glanced at the clock to check how much time we had left, then tugged gently on her hair to get her attention.

"Don't have a lot of time left, baby. Either you tell him or I will."

Blakely scrunched up her nose in annoyance, and I raised an eyebrow. She hadn't wanted to tell him what happened with her foster family, but I knew he would be livid if Saber heard about it from someone else. I needed to make sure that he was calm when he went back to his cell and didn't do anything stupid that would keep him from getting parole someday.

His eyes narrowed, and he glanced back and forth between me and Blakely. "Tell me what?"

She sighed. "There was this thing..."

As she explained what happened, Saber's face darkened with rage, and I glanced at the guard standing nearby, hoping he didn't notice. Luckily, his attention was on another inmate.

"Relax, Saber," I murmured.

"Relax?" he growled. "I'm gonna k—"

"It's taken care of." I cut him off from announcing to everyone that he was gonna murder someone else.

"Taken care of?" His hand slashed through the air in a gesture of frustration. "She's staying at the club. I trust my boys with my life but not with my daughter."

"Agreed. Which is why I've been staying with her while the situation was handled."

Saber's gaze bounced between me and Blakely again, but he seemed to be fighting to accept what he clearly saw right in front of him.

"I should be handling this shit," he grunted.

Shaking my head, I said, "Even if you weren't behind bars, this would be mine to deal with."

Saber scowled, and if I were a lesser man, I could see how he had people shaking in their boots and ran his MC with an iron fist. But if he thought he could intimidate me...he had another thing coming. "She's my daughter," he insisted.

"And she's my woman."

Blakely gasped, and her elbow hit me in the stomach, though the impact didn't faze me. "You weren't supposed to say that!" she hissed. "You agreed—"

"Did I?" I kept my gaze locked on her father's. On our way to the prison, she'd asked me not to tell him just yet. I'd made a noncommittal grunt, not giving her an answer either way. I had no intention of keeping it to myself, but I didn't want to upset her right before we went in to see her dad.

Blakely sputtered for a few seconds, then huffed. "Daddy, I can explain. It's—"

"Baby, he doesn't need an explanation. He knows exactly what's going on."

"I don't see a vest," he growled, though his glare had lost some of its heat.

"It'll be waiting for her when we get home."

"Um, what?" Blakely gasped, but I ignored her for the moment.

"I expect you to wait until I get out for the wedding."

I narrowed my eyes. "Not a chance in hell."

Saber grinned smugly. "That's what I thought."

Blakely sputtered again, and I finally looked in her direction and winked with a smirk. "W-we-did you say—"

"Breathe, baby," I told her soothingly as I rubbed slow circles on her back. "We'll talk about it later."

"You could do worse, pretty girl."

Something about the look in his eyes and his tone caused a niggling in the back of my brain.

The guard called out that it was time for the prisoners to say their goodbyes, and Saber's expression remained smug when he stood.

"See you soon, pretty girl," he murmured to Blakely.

When he swung his gaze back to me, I gave him a chin lift. "I'll take care of her."

"I knew you would," he mumbled as he stood and turned to walk back to the guard.

What the fuck?

I replayed what had just happened in my head.

Well, shit.

A smile slowly crawled across my face as the realization hit me. That asshole had known I'd fallen for Blakely, which was why he'd convinced me to stay in her life rather than letting someone else take over her protection.

I captured Blakely's hand in mine, and we retrieved our IDs before walking out into the sunshine.

"Are you going to explain what just happened?" she blurted as she shoved some of her blond tresses out of her face and stared up at me with wide, blue eyes.

"Your dad just gave us his blessing."

"For what?"

I laughed and planted a kiss on her lips that left her in a daze.

"Everything, baby."

"ARE you going to explain what you and my dad were talking about?" Blakely huffed when we returned to the clubhouse.

I sighed and grabbed her waist, then set her on the dresser and stepped between her legs. "I didn't want to do this here, but I guess that's what I get for ambushing you by telling your dad about us."

"Too freaking right," she said with a sniff, making me laugh. Damn, she was cute.

"You know what it means when a man gives his woman a vest."

"I do. But tell me anyway." Her eyes were apprehensive but filled with hope.

I grinned. She didn't want to misunderstand the situation, and I couldn't blame her. So I laid it out as plain as day. "I love you, Blakely. Have since long before I should've. When we get home, you're gonna wear my property patch, marry me, and give me babies."

Blakely blinked a few times, digesting what I'd said. Then a beautiful smile lit up her face, and she threw her arms around me. "I love you, too!"

"I know, baby." I slipped a hand into the hair at the back of her skull and tugged it to draw her head back, giving me access to her mouth. "You're gonna marry me," I said against her mouth. It wasn't a question.

"Yes," she panted.

Her legs had curled around my hips, so I slipped my hands under her ass and held her to me as I turned and stalked to the bed. When I dropped her onto the mattress, her laughter sent warmth flooding through my body.

"Now," I growled as I took off my vest and stripped out of my shirt. "About making those babies..."

EPILOGUE
BLAKELY

G lancing down at my phone's screen at the text notification, I smiled when I saw Molly's name. Everyone had welcomed me with open arms when Gideon had brought me to Old Bridge, but the VP's old lady held a special place in my heart. She was awesome and had been so much help in getting me settled into my new life with the Iron Rogues.

Tapping on the screen, I let out a shriek when I read her message.

MOLLY

Come over to the shop. Someone just brought a baby to Whiskey!

"What's going on?" Elise asked.

Gideon's sister and I had been baking a batch of triple chocolate chip cookies. Luckily, we had just pulled the last dozen out of the oven so we could head over to Iron Inkworks to see what was happening.

Showing her the text from Molly, I stripped off the apron I had been wearing.

"Holy crap," she squealed, heading for the door. "Hurry up, let's go."

We hurried down a couple of blocks to the tattoo parlor owned by the Iron Rogues as a prospect trailed us. Gideon and Blade were out taking care of something for Fox, so he'd been tasked with keeping an eye on us until they got back to the clubhouse later tonight.

"Do you think Whiskey got someone pregnant and is just now finding out he has a baby?" I asked.

"Doubt that," the prospect muttered. "Never seen him with a woman before."

"Yeah, he doesn't seem like the type to me," Elise agreed.

I nodded, thinking the same thing. But when we pushed open the door of the tattoo parlor, Molly's message was confirmed. Whiskey was pacing back and forth in the waiting area, holding an infant who looked no more than a few weeks old. Dressed in a navy-blue pantsuit with a white button-down shirt, the woman standing next to him didn't look like a baby mama. Plus, her gray hair and wrinkles put her outside her childbearing years.

I wondered if she was the mom's mother, but then she handed Whiskey a business card and said, "Please call me if you have any questions. Someone from the local children's services offices will follow up with you since I'm handing the case over to one of their social workers."

"What happened?" I asked Molly when she padded over to us.

"I'm not sure," she whispered, her gaze sympathetic as she glanced at Whiskey over her shoulder. "The only thing I caught was that his sister is the mom."

Elise shook her head. "I didn't even know he had any siblings."

"Same, so they're definitely not close," Dahlia added as she joined us. If anyone was in the know about the guys, it was her since she was the president's old lady.

The baby started crying again as soon as the woman left the shop. She looked so tiny cradled in Whiskey's tattooed, muscular arms as he bounced her against his broad chest. "Fuck, I have a client coming in for their second session on a full sleeve in ten minutes. What the hell am I gonna do?"

Dahlia rushed over to him to take the baby from his arms. "Don't worry, I can watch her for today."

"And we've already started stocking up on baby stuff, so she can borrow some things while one of the prospects runs out to grab anything else she needs," Molly added.

Pulling my phone out of my pocket, I offered, "I can work on a list so he'll know what to get."

"Thanks," Whiskey muttered. "That'll work for the short-term, but I guess I'm gonna need to find a fucking nanny."

Elise clapped her hands, bouncing on the balls of her feet. "Ohhhh, I know the perfect person! I met her last week at the library."

Whiskey narrowed his eyes at her, but his voice was gentle as he said, "So you barely know this chick?"

"I mean, I'm sure you'll run a background check on her, but she was volunteering while she was there." Elise beamed a smile at him. "And I already know that she loves kids because she was reading to a huge group of them. I asked how often she does it because she's amazing, and she's there twice a week.

The librarian said they wished they could offer her a full-time job doing it because the daycare center where she's worked since she was a sophomore in high school just shut down, and now she's without a job right when she graduated. A whole semester early."

"Damn, girl." Molly let out an appreciative whistle. "You practically got her entire life story."

Dahlia rocked the baby back and forth. "And she sounds like she'd be the perfect nanny."

"I guess we'll find out," Whiskey conceded as his appointment walked in the door.

As we headed over to the clubhouse, Elise rubbed her palms together. "I'm willing to bet she'll be perfect as more than just the nanny."

"Well played," Molly congratulated with a soft laugh.

"This is so wild." Dahlia shook her head. "I never would've guessed Whiskey would end up being a single daddy."

"Everything is turning up babies around here," I murmured, resting my hand over my still-flat belly.

"Oh my gosh," Elise squealed. "You're pregnant too!"

"Yup." I beamed a smile at her. "Our due dates

shouldn't be too far apart, so our children will grow up more like siblings than cousins."

"With three other bonus cousins in their Iron Rogues family," Molly added, gesturing at her and her sister's rounded bellies. "Now that we've got this little one here."

EPILOGUE
STORM

"Don't know if I'll ever be able to be inside this room without getting hard as fuck," I murmured to Blakely as we walked into the room we used when we'd stayed with the Westland Riders. The one her dad had said he'd never return to when he found out it was the one Jagger had put her in when we got together. One of the prospects had moved his shit to another room, and this one was ours whenever we visited.

Blakely's cheeks heated, and I couldn't help smiling at how adorable she was. All the years we'd been together, all the things we'd done and said, and she still blushed like a virgin at the topic of sex.

I curled my arm around her waist and pulled her body against mine, bucking my hips so she could feel every inch of my long, rigid cock. "The kids are with Staci until tonight," I grunted as I glided a hand under her skirt. I fucking loved it when she wore skirts and dresses. "Should I remind you how it felt when I popped your cherry and made you mine?"

Blakely moaned, and her hands tunneled into my hair. "Yes, please."

Feeling the tiny string holding up her panties, I snapped it and ripped them away. "Maybe I'll even get you pregnant again."

"Gideon," Blakely groaned. "I'm still nursing Cobi. I—oh!"

She stopped talking when I tossed her on the bed and dropped to my knees, latching my mouth onto her drenched pussy. "Always so fucking wet for me," I grunted as I ate her like she was my last meal.

After driving her to one screaming orgasm, I quickly stripped us both and climbed onto the bed. I laid on my back and guided her up so she was straddling me on her knees. Her tits glistened with beads of milk, and I knifed up to lick each tip before sucking one into my mouth.

"Gideon!" she called out as she dropped down onto my cock.

"Fuck!" I shouted at the tight grip of her pussy. "Ride me, Blakely. That's my good girl. Fuck, yes!"

My hips immediately took up a steady rhythm, fucking up into her slick channel. "Always love fucking you, baby. But damn, tasting your milky tits while you bounce on my cock is...oh fuck, yeah!" I groaned when she squeezed me, and her inner muscles rippled around my dick.

I sat up again and gave her other breast attention, drinking her sweetness until I was ready to break.

Falling back onto the mattress, I gripped her hips, helping her up and down so I was slamming up into her every time she came crashing down. "Yes! Fuck! That's my gorgeous girl. Taking me so good."

I suddenly flipped us over and pushed her legs back into her chest, shoving my dick in so deep, I bumped her womb. "Tell me you want my baby, Blakely," I grunted. Her inner muscles spasmed, and I grinned. "Yeah, that's what I thought. Tell me. Tell me you want me to fuck another baby into you."

"Yes," she moaned, her head thrashing as her body writhed beneath me.

"Say it, baby."

"I want you to fuck me!"

Come spurted from my cock, but I wasn't ready to let go. "And?"

She opened her beautiful blue eyes and stared

into my gaze as she whispered, "Give me your baby, Gideon."

"That's my good girl."

Just like the night I made her mine, I fucked her long, hard, and deep. The bed crashed into the wall over and over while she chanted, "Yes! Yes! Oh yes, Gideon!"

My spine tingled, and I knew I was about to lose it, so I reached between us and pinched her clit. She screamed my name as her climax hit her, and I exploded right after.

"Fuck, yes!" I roared as I pumped my come into her womb, stuffing her full and silently ordering my boys to do their job.

An hour later, I'd fucked her once more for good measure. We were lying in our blissed-out state, trying to catch our breath, when she glanced at the clock and shrieked, "We have to be there in an hour!"

"Calm down, baby. The prison is only forty minutes away." Blakely's dad was getting out, and we'd come down to be there when he walked out a free man.

"I don't have time to shower," she whined.

"So?" I was distracted watching her round, delicious ass as she climbed out of bed.

"I'm not meeting my father smelling like sex with your come dripping down my thighs!"

I couldn't help it. I burst out laughing at the adorably put-out expression on her face. "Baby, no one but you and me are gonna know I just stuffed you full of my jizz if you wear panties."

Blakely threw her hands in the air and growled, "You ruined them, you big caveman!"

Oh...right. I shrugged. "Grab a pair from your suitcase, baby."

She growled adorably again. "Then I won't have enough to last the time we're here. Ugh, Stop ruining all of my underwear."

"You'll just have to go commando on the way home," I told her with a grin.

She put her hands on her hips and smirked at me. "The kids will be in the car, Gideon. No easy access for you."

I frowned. *Damn.* Our kids were awesome, but they were the world's best cockblockers. "I'll just have to fuck you long and hard before we leave to get me through," I teased her with a wicked smile.

Blakely laughed, and I stared at the beautiful sight, still amazed that she was mine.

"I love you, baby."

Her expression turned soft. "Love you, too. Now

get your sexy butt outta that bed before I climb you like a tree."

I growled as I hopped off the mattress. "You can't say shit like that when I can't..."

She giggled and dashed past me before I could get my arms around her. Then she ran around picking up her clothes.

"I see my good little girl decided to be naughty today."

Blakely's cheeks turned pink, and I shook my head.

"Naughty girls get spanked, Blakely."

She winked. "I know."

Curious about Whiskey and the nanny he's going to hire? Find out what happens in Whiskey!

And if you join our newsletter, you'll get an email from us with a link to claim a FREE copy of The Virgin's Guardian, which was banned on Amazon.

ABOUT THE AUTHOR

The writing duo of Elle Christensen and Rochelle Paige team up under the Fiona Davenport pen name to bring you sexy, insta-love stories filled with alpha males. If you want a quick & dirty read with a guaranteed happily ever after, then give Fiona Davenport a try!

⬚ ⬚ ⬚ ⬚

Printed in Great Britain
by Amazon